S0-BZC-965

Praise for Liz Allison and Wendy Etherington

"There is action, drama, romance
and a touch of suspense, and the characters
are charming, realistic and very engaging."
—*The Romance Readers Connection*
on *Risking Her Heart*

"*No Holding Back* is a wonderful introduction
to the racing world and an even better romantic read."
—*Fresh Fiction*

"The best yet.
The main characters' emotional struggles to find love
and contentment are heart-achingly depicted."
—*RT Book Reviews* on *Winning It All*

Praise for Abby Gaines

"Abby Gaines isn't afraid to pen a romance
that deals with real-life problems…
poignant…humorous and touching."
—*RT Book Reviews* on *Fully Engaged*

"[Gaines] has a real talent for sparkling dialogue."
—*RT Book Reviews* on *Her So-Called Fiancé*

JUN 0 3 2010

LIZ ALLISON

married into NASCAR in 1989 when the second-generation driver Davey Allison stole her heart. Though Liz's life took a tragic turn in 1993 when Davey was killed in a helicopter accident, Liz has continued to share her love and passion for racing by hosting TV and radio shows, as well as authoring books about America's fastest-growing sport. Liz lives in Nashville with her husband, Ryan, and three children, Robbie, Krista and Bella.

WENDY ETHERINGTON

was born and raised in the deep South—and she has the fried-chicken recipes and NASCAR ticket stubs to prove it. She has nearly twenty published novels to her credit and has been a finalist for many awards, including several *RT Book Reviews* awards. She writes full-time from her home in South Carolina, where she lives with her husband and two daughters.

ABBY GAINES

Like some of her favorite NASCAR drivers, Abby Gaines's first love was open-wheel dirt track racing. As editor of a speedway magazine, she spent many summer evenings at her favorite local track. Now, Abby's thrilled to combine her love of NASCAR with her love of writing. In addition to the Harlequin NASCAR series, Abby also writes novels for Harlequin Superromance. She lives with her husband, her three children, a labradoodle and, the most demanding member of the household, a haughty black cat. Visit Abby at www.abbygaines.com, or e-mail her at abby@abbygaines.com and let her know if you enjoyed this story.

NASCAR®

The Memory of a Kiss

Liz Allison & Wendy Etherington ∾ Abby Gaines

HARLEQUIN®

TORONTO • NEW YORK • LONDON
AMSTERDAM • PARIS • SYDNEY • HAMBURG
STOCKHOLM • ATHENS • TOKYO • MILAN • MADRID
PRAGUE • WARSAW • BUDAPEST • AUCKLAND

If you purchased this book without a cover you should be aware that this book is stolen property. It was reported as "unsold and destroyed" to the publisher, and neither the author nor the publisher has received any payment for this "stripped book."

ISBN-13: 978-0-373-18535-1

THE MEMORY OF A KISS

Copyright © 2010 by Harlequin Books S.A.

Recycling programs for this product may not exist in your area.

The publisher acknowledges the copyright holders of the individual works as follows:

LONG GONE
Copyright © 2010 by Harlequin Books S.A.
Liz Allison and Wendy Etherington are acknowledged as the authors of "Long Gone."

CHASING THE DREAM
Copyright © 2010 by Harlequin Books S.A.
Abby Gaines is acknowledged as the author of "Chasing the Dream."

NASCAR® and the NASCAR Library Collection® are registered trademarks of the National Association for Stock Car Auto Racing, Inc.

All rights reserved. Except for use in any review, the reproduction or utilization of this work in whole or in part in any form by any electronic, mechanical or other means, now known or hereafter invented, including xerography, photocopying and recording, or in any information storage or retrieval system, is forbidden without the written permission of the publisher, Harlequin Enterprises Limited, 225 Duncan Mill Road, Don Mills, Ontario, Canada M3B 3K9.

This is a work of fiction. Names, characters, places and incidents are either the product of the author's imagination or are used fictitiously, and any resemblance to actual persons, living or dead, business establishments, events or locales is entirely coincidental.

This edition published by arrangement with Harlequin Books S.A.

® and TM are trademarks of the publisher. Trademarks indicated with ® are registered in the United States Patent and Trademark Office, the Canadian Trade Marks Office and in other countries.

www.eHarlequin.com

Printed in U.S.A.

CONTENTS

PROLOGUE   7
An excerpt from Hilton Branch's journal

LONG GONE   11
Liz Allison and Wendy Etherington

CHASING THE DREAM   97
Abby Gaines

An excerpt from Hilton Branch's prison journal...

This journal the prison shrink told me to start after the heart attack—what am I supposed to write? She says start with the beginning, but hell, I've lived it all. I don't need any reminders.

She says it will help, but maybe it's really only my punishment, to have to face all I've done. There are many sins on my head, a lot of secrets no one knows. I never meant to fall in love—certainly not with a woman so much younger, a widow with a teenager already—but there was such sweetness in Rose, the fresh air and joy she brought into my life. Yes, I was already married to Maeve with four grown children, but when Rose turned up pregnant with my baby—her, an old-fashioned girl who'd expect her baby's father to marry her—what was I to do?

She didn't know my real name. Thought I had to travel for a living. Heaven knows I wished nearly every day of that time that I was an ordinary man with a simple job who could just come home to her every night.

A man like my father. I grew up poor in East Texas, and I knew early on that being like my dad, scared of his own shadow, was to end up the same way. I wanted more. I never liked being told what to do. I do better being in charge. I worked my ass off to be a success, and I was. Made more money than most people ever dream of.

Yet here I am, flat broke. A dead-end job in the prison bakery, for God's sake—me, Hilton Branch, who once gave orders to hundreds of people and was the envy of all of Texas.

But I had my two sons' race teams to sponsor, millions of dollars a year for Will and Bart. The mansion in Dallas, the condo in Charlotte, the planes I bought my boys. Maeve never held a job, wouldn't know how. Rose, she'd worked herself nearly to the bone, so it was my honor to give her the chance to stay home with her children as she'd always yearned to do.

Then there was Alyssa, she-cat mistress with her claws dug straight into my belly. Twenty years ought to entitle a man to some peace, but there was none with that one, no, sir.

I made a bundle in my day, but it was never enough. I had to siphon off funds from BMT, but it was my damn company, wasn't it? My old buddy and business partner, Fred Clifton, didn't think so. The price of his silence was buying him out...and I got the money the only way I could, under the table. Biscayne Bay Holding Company, operating out of the Caribbean. They didn't pass the smell test, but by then, I didn't have any options.

When they got impatient for payments I couldn't make, well...I had to run. Pulled money out of every possible source and left the country. Hid like a common criminal— me, Hilton Branch!

The worst part of it was having to leave Rose. Having to lie to her about where I was and when I'd be back.

Which turned out to be never.

Thank God she can't see me like this. Better she think me dead.

But I do love you, Rose. Like I never knew was possible.

Long Gone

Liz Allison and Wendy Etherington

CHAPTER ONE

DANE GUTHRIE STOOD in a shadowed corner of the over-crowded room, watching the party atmosphere around him roll as smoothly as his team pushed the race car around the infield garage. He, however, found the whole experience tedious, bordering on ridiculous.

Small talk, tiny topics, forced smiles and too-perfect clothes. He was as uncomfortable and out of place as a set of square tires.

"Come on, man," Bart Branch said, walking toward him with a pair of beer bottles in his hand, one of which he handed to Dane. "It's a party, remember?"

The successful NASCAR driver, who was the veteran at Dane's new team, PDQ Racing, had been glad to have him onboard, but had already decided he needed to lighten up and wouldn't hear that Dane didn't have a choice about being serious. He just was.

"How could I forget?" Dane asked, his sarcasm obvious.

"You could at least act like you're having a good time for my sponsor's sake."

Sponsors. They were the reason Dane had been tapped, along with Bart's PR rep, to attend the event in the first place. PDQ's owner, Jim Latimer, was representing them at another party, so he'd been unable to attend. With so much going on the week before the season-opening races in Daytona, the staff was stretched thin. Obviously. Only desperation would lead Jim to send Dane as company representative for a social occasion. He was a damn crew chief, not a marketing guru.

Still the people at EZ-Plus Software, Bart's sponsor, had gone to a lot of trouble to attract press, NASCAR insiders and their customers.

They'd rented out an entire restaurant and filled it not only with people but with three bars and several tables loaded with appetizers, desserts and even a chocolate fountain. White lights flickered on every available surface, even dangling from the ceiling, and balloons in Bart's colors of red and orange bobbed in the corners like buoys in the sea.

Drinks in hand as they talked in small groups or hovered around the food tables, everyone seemed to be enjoying themselves.

Except him.

Drawing a resigned sigh, Dane focused on Bart. With his blond good looks and bright baby blues, he was a hit with women. His intelligence and dedication made him equally popular with guys. Sponsors and fans loved it all.

"I didn't get a chance to talk to your crew after practice," Dane began. "How'd things go?"

Bart grinned as if he knew talking about work was the only kind of chatting Dane was capable of. "We ran well in the draft. I'm not sure how great we'll qualify, though. How'd Kelsey do?"

Dane's rookie driver had come over this season from open-wheel racing. That transition was a challenge in itself, but press, colleagues and experts often considered her just a pretty face and questioned her ability to win in NASCAR.

"She stayed relatively calm. She didn't wreck herself or anybody else," Dane said.

"That's success the first time at Daytona. She'll get the hang of it."

Despite the naysayers, Bart was encouraging, classy and respectful toward Kelsey. Both Dane and his driver were grateful to have such a supportive teammate. "She's listened to your advice. That's helped a lot. I think the criticism and intense press has gotten to her a little."

"Yeah, well, I guess I know something about that, too. At least they're talking about her driving ability, not what her idiotic father has done lately."

Dane was a bit surprised by the bitterness in Bart's voice, even though he supposed the other man had a right. His father, Hilton, was currently in prison, serving a twenty-year sentence for bank fraud and embezzlement. He'd been a fugitive for the better part of a year, he'd been caught in a long-term affair, he'd cheated his customers, his family and his employees out of both their reputations and millions of dollars, and all of it had been splashed endlessly across every media outlet available.

"She has to learn to block that stuff out," Dane said, figuring he didn't know Bart well enough to ask him how things were going with his family—even if he knew what to say. "If she can focus on driving, she'll do well, and everything else will follow."

They moved on to talking about handling, whose car among the competition looked good or lousy, and after a few minutes, Kelsey walked over and joined their conversation. For the first time all night, Dane relaxed. He was content talking about drafting, tires, restrictor plates and straightaway speeds. These were things he expected, he could calculate and strategize about.

"Hello, gorgeous."

That voice, however, was unexpected.

As he watched Kelsey's eyes widen with surprise and pleasure, then Bart's spark with interest, he closed his own.

He hadn't heard that voice live in over fourteen years. Recorded in high-tech digital sound, he'd sat in many dark rooms, wondered about the past and the present, and let her words soothe his soul. The continued weakness after so much pain was a part of him he both resented and would never admit.

Bracing himself, he turned to face Lizzie Lancaster.

With her tall, slender body, fiery hair and deep-blue-ocean eyes, she was as stunning as her pictures, different than he remembered in person. She was more polished, wore more makeup and less clothes. In a sparkly silver dress, with miles of sleek, tanned legs exposed, she lit up the room and stood out clearly as a superstar. Even in the presence of several.

Before he could say a word, she pulled him into a tight hug, brushing her lips over his cheek as she leaned back. "It's been a long time."

The scent of her exotic-smelling perfume and the warmth of her mouth lingered even after they were no longer touching. His stomach clenched.

"Yeah," he managed to say, clearly recalling the rainy spring afternoon he'd watched her climb on a bus and roll out of town and out of his life.

"I'm a big fan," Bart said, after a quick, surprised glance at Dane. Clearly his cool quotient had gone up if he warranted a hug from Lizzie Lancaster.

"Oh, yeah?" Lizzie smiled widely at Bart. "Same to you."

While Bart and Kelsey gushed over Lizzie, and she introduced the various people surrounding her—a manager, a publicist *and* an assistant—Dane said little. Not that he was ever talkative, but at the moment he could hardly hear his own thoughts over his heart's pounding.

What was she doing here?

Watching the girl he used to love—the one he thought he'd spend his life with—as she flirted with Bart, chatted with Kelsey and drew every eye in the room to her was physically painful. She'd made him vulnerable to that pain. A weakness he'd sworn he'd never feel again.

He didn't belong at this party. He'd never belonged with her.

Of course, the drivers easily captured her attention, and Dane was happy to hover in the background.

"I heard you're singing the national anthem before the race next Sunday," Kelsey said.

What? Obviously, this was the one time he probably should have pulled his head out from under the hood of his race car and paid attention to a press release.

"It's a big honor," Lizzie said. Her gaze met Dane's. "A long way from the press box at the local short tracks."

"You're a race fan?" Bart asked.

"Sure. Dane and I went to high school together near Myrtle Beach, and you couldn't be around him without following racing."

"Oh, yeah?" Bart's eyes grew speculative. "High school sweethearts, huh?"

"We were, as a matter of fact," Lizzie said.

The smile slid off Bart's face, replaced by disbelief, mirroring Dane's own feelings. They were total opposites. He certainly couldn't picture himself with the woman she'd become.

And yet, here they were, standing less than a foot apart, and all he wanted to do was run in the opposite direction.

He gripped his beer bottle and fought the impulse to do just that. "It was a lifetime ago."

As LIZZIE STARED at the living embodiment of her past—and the hard, closed expression on his handsome face—she found herself filled with regrets for the first time in a very long time.

Hadn't she boarded a bus to Nashville with nothing, and hadn't she made her dreams come true with her music career? Hadn't she been honored with awards and platinum-selling CDs?

Staring at Dane, she found it hard to believe he could see her after so many years and still be angry. She couldn't possibly have hurt him more than he had her. She lifted her chin. "It certainly was."

So why was she letting a guy she'd known long ago shake her confidence and force her to question the choices she'd made?

Her decision had been the right one. If she'd stayed with Dane, she'd likely be married with kids and driving a minivan by now. Would she really trade that life over all she'd accomplished?

True, there were times she missed him, missed the wide-eyed, adolescent love they shared and wondered what might have been. She'd be cured once she moved on to the next stop in her tour.

But, for now, the second thoughts were there, lurking.

She linked her arm with Bart's. His uncomplicated flirting was much easier to deal with. "So, my staff and I have a pool going on the race. Should I bet on you?"

Bart puffed out his chest. "Absolutely."

Lizzie squeezed his arm. He was adorable. The exact opposite of the silent and intense Dane. She glanced over at Kelsey. "I don't know, maybe us women stick together."

"My crew chief here is certainly confident," Kelsey said, shrugging. "And I haven't wrecked anything yet."

"He always was a sharp guy," Lizzie said, shifting her attention toward Dane, searching for any sign he felt the same stomach fluttering she did.

He simply looked bored.

She suddenly wished she'd resisted the urge to come to him. The need to simply stand near him again. After all they'd been through together and apart, she'd wanted to see his reaction to her. Either because of her feminine ego or the memory of her broken teenage heart, she wanted to know if he ever thought of her.

Shaking away the need, she concentrated on what

Bart was saying. Even if Dane had issued the ultimatum, she was the one who'd made the decision to leave.
She didn't have to convince anyone that she was happy
with her life and that leaving him had been worth it.

If only she could convince herself.

CHAPTER TWO

A REP FROM EZ-Plus Software joined the circle, saving Dane from having to comment on his confidence in winning the race.

Because she knew him so well, Lizzie figured she was the only one who saw relief jump into his vivid green eyes as the conversation moved away from him and onto the party.

"Do you want some champagne?" her assistant, Maggie, asked in her ear.

Grateful, Lizzie nodded while the EZ-Plus guy explained how impressed he'd been with the light show on her latest concert tour.

"I told Lizzie that would be the highlight of the show," Ronnie Filmore, her manager, said with a wink to the group.

"And here I thought people came to hear me sing," Lizzie said dryly.

At her comment, a hint of a smile appeared on Dane's lips. Which, unfortunately, disappeared the moment he realized Lizzie was watching him.

The man was as aloof and rigid as the English butler Ronnie had hired to watch over her Nashville estate. He was supposed to "class up the place," according to

Ronnie. But if the house's over-the-top twelve thousand square feet alone didn't give her class, then Lizzie was personally out of ideas.

"It's all about layering, darling," Ronnie said with an expressive wave of his hand, the heavy ruby ring he always wore flashing beneath the lights. "You need the voice of a generation *and* great lighting." He winked and everyone laughed.

Everybody knew Ronnie was a great manager. The trouble was, Ronnie knew it better than anybody.

And while Lizzie appreciated confidence—singers didn't perform in front of fifty thousand fans without oodles of it—she was less patient with arrogance. Even less tolerant of bragging.

But wasn't that Ronnie's job? To promote her and manage her career?

She was just feeling out of sorts because of Dane. He'd attracted her, distracted her and annoyed her all in the space of ten minutes.

And it occurred to her at that moment that Dane would hate Ronnie.

A quick glance at her ex confirmed the thought. He managed to look aggravated, scornful and bored all at the same time.

Gorgeous, too. Don't forget gorgeous, Lizzie.

Maggie pressed a glass of champagne into her hand, bringing Lizzie abruptly back to the discussion—which had moved on to the merits of dry ice machines on stage.

"Thanks," Lizzie said to her assistant, then took a bracing sip of the sparkling wine.

"Of course fog won't save you from a lousy voice,"

Ronnie said knowingly. "Remember Paula Jermaine opening for your tour last fall?"

Lizzie sent Ronnie a warning look, which he ignored.

"Apparently," he continued, his voice dropping low so that the others had to lean in to hear him, "that hit song she had was all studio magic. I sing better than her in the shower. And, trust me, that's not sayin' much."

"She's just young, Ronnie," Lizzie said.

Ronnie rolled on as if she hadn't spoken. "Her people decided to have her come up through the floor of the stage, surrounded by fog." He shook his head. "Unfortunately, she started coughing, and honey, please, that did *not* do anything for her lousy voice."

Everybody laughed—well, except for Dane—and Lizzie felt uncomfortable.

"Cut it out, Ronnie," she said. "We're surrounded by race people, and we're going on and on about the music business. I'm sure they'd much rather talk about the exhibition race coming up tomorrow night."

The group exchanged uncertain looks.

What was with them? All Dane had ever talked about, thought about or planned for was racing. And everybody around him seemed to be cut from the same cloth.

"Actually," Kelsey began, breaking the uncomfortable silence, "I'd love to know what James Allenton is like. Is he really that hot in person?"

Ignoring Ronnie's triumphant grin and resigned to industry gossip, Lizzie assured Kelsey that, yes, James was that hot.

She managed to keep the discussion mostly positive—even though Ronnie tried to derail her several times. She wasn't about to spread ugly rumors about fellow artists. Her community was too close-knit. Nashville was a country music town the way Mooresville, North Carolina, was a racing town, and it never helped a career to be the one always stirring up trouble.

Bart's PR rep, Anita Wolcott-Latimer, joined the group, but only long enough for introductions. She needed Bart and Kelsey to mingle with the sponsors. The EZ-Plus rep left with them, leaving Lizzie with Dane and her staff.

Seemingly of its own accord, her gaze connected with her ex's. The banked heat she found there—most likely due to anger—challenged her to find the source and purge it.

"Could I have a few minutes alone with Dane, guys?" she asked her staff.

They murmured their agreement and wandered away, though Ronnie sent her a wink and a thumbs-up before he was swallowed up by the crowd.

Saying nothing, she and Dane stared at each other.

Though she was tall for a woman, Dane dwarfed her. At six-four, with broad shoulders, piercing green eyes and a serious expression, most women would be intimidated by him. She, on the other hand, remembered a lanky teenager, determined to prove himself to her and the world.

"So," she said casually, placing her hand on her cocked hip, "how've you been?"

He looked surprised by her pleasant tone. "You're kidding, right?"

"No. It's been fourteen years since I've seen you or talked to you. I'd like to know how you've been doing." She forced a smile. "It's called civilized conversation."

"I don't like conversation."

"I remember." She vividly recalled heated glances and seeking hands. "You were more physical."

"*You* talked," he said shortly, as if it were an unforgivable character flaw.

"My voice is my power."

He raised his eyebrows. "You get that from some fancy philosophical guru?"

"No, I pretty much knew that at eight."

"When you won the talent competition at the mall."

"See, you haven't forgotten all about me."

"How could I? You ran out on me."

"I—" Words failed her momentarily. Leave it to Dane to skip over the small talk and get to the heart of the matter. "You demanded I choose between you and my dreams of a music career."

"You can't raise a family on the road."

His unyielding attitude hadn't changed a bit. "Plenty of people do it. In racing, in entertainment. You just didn't want to try."

Eyes as cold as an emerald, he leaned toward her. "You wanted to sell CDs more than you wanted me."

Maybe she had. Maybe she'd been as uncompromising as he had. Even through her anger and devastation, she'd questioned her decision many times. She'd even purged it in a song. But she thought she'd come to peace with the path she'd chosen.

Until tonight. Until she'd seen him, so strong and remote. The same and yet a virtual stranger. The man she'd once loved; a man she didn't recognize.

She'd expected to see him at some point over the next two weeks, but she still hadn't been prepared for the moment she'd touched him again. When her heart had jumped. When her knees had turned to jelly.

Had she been kidding herself that she'd let the old feelings go? Had she really thought they could sit down to a casual chat about old times without the pain of the past simmering in every word?

Looking at him now, she realized something beyond her own hurt and confusion—she wasn't the only one with regrets. He'd been hiding his own pain by keeping his distance.

"I'm surprised you're still so pissed off at me after fourteen long years," she said, careful to keep her tone even in contrast to his resentment. "Why do you think that is? Unresolved feelings maybe?"

DANE NEARLY TOOK A STEP backward from the confident accusation in Lizzie's eyes. Instead, he fought to look unconcerned. "I'm not pissed off. I don't think of you at all anymore."

It was a lie, but he wasn't about to admit the truth.

She crossed her arms over her chest. "Is that so?"

He mirrored her position. "Yes."

For a half a second, she seemed flustered, then she leaned toward him and drew the tip of her finger across his bare forearm. "What a shame. I think about you."

No way he could miss the smoky, seductive note in her voice. How many times had he heard it whispered in his ear as a teen, then, later, on the radio and in his dreams? She could entice anyone she wanted with a simple change in her tone.

Her fortune. His weakness.

He needed to escape her ASAP before he was pulled under again, and the heart she'd shredded by leaving was torn open again.

"I don't see how you have time," he said. "You must be too busy with your fans."

"Are you one?"

"One what?"

"A fan."

He was wary of the simple question. "I used to like to hear you sing."

She cocked her head. "Not anymore?"

He shrugged. "Haven't heard you in a while." At least not since last night, when he'd fallen asleep, listening to her latest hit on his MP3 player. "Maybe success has soured your pitch."

"Soured my—" She halted her spurt of outrage and smiled. "Clever. You always were smart. But insulting me won't get you out of this discussion."

"I could just leave."

"Sure you could." And she looked way too sure that he wouldn't.

As much as he wanted to escape her and the memories she invoked, there was something desperate, terrible and glorious about standing next to her again. People milled around them, full of conversation and laughter, but, as always, a spotlight shone on Lizzie.

"Come on, Dane," she said, her tone inviting. "You're not even a little curious about what I've been doing the last fourteen years?"

"You're all over the TV and radio. I think I can follow the dots."

She waved her hand in dismissal. "That's publicity. I'm talking about personal stuff."

"I've seen pictures of you and James Allenton."

"That's publicity, too." She shrugged. "Well, mostly. It's all a little silly sometimes, but—" She stopped, her gaze jumping to his and realization with it. "Hang on. James and I weren't ever photographed for a racing magazine. How'd you see us?"

"Ah…newspaper?"

"We wouldn't have appeared on the sports page. You read some other section?"

"Ah…sure. Sometimes."

"That's a big, fat lie," she said, poking her finger into his shoulder. "Your life is racing. Maybe you check out college basketball scores sometimes, but that's it."

"I've changed," he claimed boldly.

"You certainly have. But not about something that basic. What's with you?"

He clenched his jaw. "I have no idea what you mean."

She gave up—for the moment—and switched topics. "Is Kelsey not a good driver?"

"She seems to be. I don't know her well. I guess we'll find out tomorrow night."

"Your parents are okay?"

"They're fine. Dad finally retired last year."

"Why are you so angry? What's your problem?"

You're my problem, he wanted to shout. But then that would mean admitting she mattered. And she did.

Way too much.

"The only problem I have is helping my rookie driver get acclimated to stock cars and figure out how to give her the best setup for her to win races."

Lizzie looked skeptical. "Uh-huh."

"You know the race isn't until next Sunday. What are you doing in Daytona now?"

"I'm shooting some footage for National Country Videos. They wanted to do a special on the opening of the new season."

"Oh, well—"

"Lizzie, darling." Her manager approached, sliding his arm around her waist. "I'm sorry, but I have to steal you away for a minute." He sent Dane an apologetic smile. "Her fans are so important to her."

"Sure," Dane said, somehow simultaneously relieved and disappointed Lizzie was leaving.

And how he could be both those things at once, he had no idea. He was never indecisive. He made split-second decisions for a living.

Lizzie was back in his life for an hour, and he was already acting weird.

Wait. Back in his life?

Superstar country music sensation Lizzie Lancaster was most definitely *not* in his life. He'd given up on that dream long ago.

"No problem," he added when Lizzie looked like she was going to argue with her manager. "The fans come first."

Any other entertainer would accept that as a compliment, but Dane didn't mean it as one, and he was sure Lizzie didn't take it that way.

Her beautiful eyes lit with flames for a moment, then she banked her anger and gave him a fake, ingratiating smile. "They certainly do. Anytime you want to become one, Dane, you just let me know. I'll have

Ronnie here send you the autographed CD of your choice." She turned away, striding off, her silver dress reflecting sparks off the decorative lights.

Still holding his now-warm beer bottle, Dane stared at her retreating back—his gaze locked on her long, slender…tanned legs. Man, she had a serious body. If he ever saw her sing in person, he wasn't sure he'd actually be able to focus on her voice. He might even—

He pressed his lips together, praying he wasn't on the verge of drooling.

Turning in the opposite direction that she'd gone, he set his beer on the nearest empty table and strode out of the party.

He needed to get a hold of his emotions. And not a hold on her.

CHAPTER THREE

As TOWERS OF LIGHTS illuminated the grand super-speedway, cameras flashed in the grandstands, and the central Florida humidity hung heavy in the air, Dane climbed onto the No. 432 PDQ Racing pit box.

His driver was anxious but ready to go. His crew had worked their butts off through practice and were pumped about the possibility of walking away with the night's prize.

The media moved up and down pit road, capturing stories, getting predictions and reactions. The frenzied crowd screamed for their favorites as powerful race cars prowled around the track behind the pace car.

Daytona Saturday night.

Since the race was a special, non-points-paying event, a limited field would compete, but that didn't diminish the desire of every team member to be the best, to see their car sail across the finish line first and spend the next week bragging about their amazing win.

Typically, Dane was one of the few not caught up in the frenzy. To him, this night meant practice for his driver and data he could use for the big race next Sunday after-noon.

Where points *did* count. And that precious, elusive

quality known as momentum that could make or break a young team's season.

In their green-and-blue Reliable Credit Company uniforms, the guys milled around behind the pit wall area below him. The war wagon where he sat contained normal garage equipment like bolts, wrenches and wires, but it also had a satellite hookup, flat-screen TV and thousands of dollars in cutting-edge computer equipment.

He adjusted his headset and cued the mike to talk to Kelsey for the first time during an official NASCAR race. "Stay calm. Be smart."

"How about I *try* to stay calm and you be the smart one?"

"Keep that sense of humor, too. You'll need it."

"Maybe I'll be up front and laughing at everybody behind me."

"If you get up front, the last thing you'll be tempted to do is laugh."

"Yeah?"

"You'll be too scared to find the funny."

"Gee, thanks for the encouragement, chief."

"Just find somebody fast to draft with, and don't do anything crazy."

"I think I can handle that."

The green flag flew moments later, and Dane settled into watching the laps unfold. Right from the beginning, the cars fanned out two and three-wide, lined up in rows, nose-to-tail, sprinting in each other's tracks like a steaming locomotive. The roaring sound and raw power made Dane's heart race, even though he'd seen the intense drama unfold hundreds of times over his career.

Kelsey's car responded well to the adjustments he

called for. And like a high-octane ballet troupe, the pit crew was smooth and efficient with their stops. But as the race progressed, Kelsey struggled.

She didn't do anything crazy, but neither did she get to the front. Veterans were reluctant to draft with rookies until they'd established themselves, and Kelsey still had a lot to prove.

In the end, she picked the wrong line to draft in and wound up finishing twenty-third out of twenty-four. Not exactly the performance Dane or owner Jim Latimer was looking for. But she did run all the laps, and she stayed relatively calm, if ultimately frustrated.

She completed the media interviews with good grace, and Dane was waiting just beyond the camera's eye to pat her back. "Let it go. You did fine."

"Fine. Yeah." She narrowed her eyes. "I didn't come to do fine. I came here to win."

"You'll get there. Get some rest before qualifying tomorrow."

She tucked her helmet beneath her arm. "Sure thing, chief. See ya."

Her frustrated stride carried her away, and though Dane still had to supervise the equipment breakdown, meet with the team and lock down the garage stall for the night, his thoughts turned to Lizzie.

During the busy preparations for the race, he'd managed to push her to the back of his mind. With the excitement and tension behind him—at least for the moment—she intruded like a thief in the night. And as hard as he tried to force her back, she simply wouldn't go.

Typical.

She'd often accused him of being stubborn. Well, he had nothing on her.

Her leaving had changed him. He wasn't a wide-eyed, trusting kid anymore. He didn't dream of the impossible. Or even the improbable. He faced reality.

The practical, meticulous man he'd become had risen to the top of racing. Why should he question decisions he'd made more than a decade ago? Why should he wonder how different his life might have been if she'd loved him more, if they'd stuck together and sacrificed everything else?

They'd have been miserable.

She had to follow her dream of music; he had to follow the road in racing. That was how it was supposed to be. And no matter the "what ifs," he couldn't change anything now.

Lizzie wouldn't be around long. He just had to avoid her until she moved on to the next stop in her glamorous lifestyle, and he'd feel normal again.

He stored the computer equipment in the hauler, then met briefly with the team. After giving report times for the morning, he let them go, while he and his car chief made sure everything was put up and secured for the night.

Walking out of the garage, he noticed a crowd of people near the back gate. Since the race was long over, and the only people left were a straggle of crew members and officials, the gathering was unusual.

As the throng inched along the area between the haulers and garage, Dane's only thought was hoping this wasn't a NASCAR official coming to announce that one of the cars inspected after the race had failed in some aspect of the rulebook. He wouldn't wish that news on any crew chief.

Well, almost none of them.

He'd started across the road between his team's garage stall and hauler when the crowd parted.

And Lizzie Lancaster walked through.

Her flaming hair pulled back in a casual ponytail, she wore jeans and a simple white T-shirt. She looked nothing like the sparkling glamour queen from the night before. Still, there was no denying her star power. A spotlight seemed to follow her every movement.

But maybe he was being fanciful.

Hang on. He was never fanciful. Hell, he'd never, in his entire life, even used the word *fanciful*. What the devil was wrong with him? What had she done to him?

Nothing.

Relieved, he noted that as she walked there was an actual spotlight following her—a portable overhead light, as well as a cameraman.

At least he hadn't completely lost all sense of himself.

Unlike *some* people.

Grown men who should have more dignity or restraint—a few of whom were even wearing the green and blue colors of the No. 432 car—held out autographed books and posed for pictures with Lizzie as if they'd never seen a celebrity in their lives. And most of them worked for sports superstars.

Dane watched the spectacle with his arms crossed over his chest. If this was some attempt by Lizzie's manager for publicity, he'd seriously missed the mark. The usual media had long since packed up. This camera crew wasn't part of the usual track coverage.

Maybe this was another bonding-with-fans opportunity. Captured on film.

But then he realized she was alone—well, except for the throngs of admirers and cameras in her wake. Her team from the night before was nowhere around. No assistant, no manager or publicist.

He narrowed his eyes. What was she up to?

His suspicions—along with his heart rate—increased when she spotted him standing on the sidelines and headed directly toward him.

"Hi," she said brightly, stopping so close a whiff of her warm, tangy perfume washed over him.

"Hi," he returned, his tone more cautious.

The guys around her stared at him in surprise. Quiet, serious Dane Guthrie knew Lizzie Lancaster? Gee, if only he'd known he could cash in the "I used to date a celebrity" card, he wouldn't have had to spend the last decade proving he was the best by winning races.

He swept the crowd with a dark glare, and pretty quickly they all found something else they needed to be doing. Somewhere else.

Lizzie spoke quietly to the camera crew, then waved them off, turning back to him. "Sorry the race didn't go well. Was Kelsey disappointed?"

"I guess. What are you doing here?"

She sighed. "Were you this rude when we were together?"

"I'm not rude. I'm direct." He shrugged. "Saves time."

"Not everything in life has to be done at 180 miles an hour."

"It does in my world, and you didn't answer the question. What are you doing here?"

"The video special, remember. Plus, I wanted to watch the race and talk to you."

"Why?"

"Because I'm apparently delusional."

He frowned. "This is a very strange conversation."

"How would you know? You never have them." She looked around, probably for an escape route. "How about I buy you a drink somewhere? We can catch up."

"Okay," he blurted without thinking.

Clearly suspicious, she repeated, "Okay?"

Part of him wanted to call the word back, but he didn't. Being near Lizzie again was both surreal and not going to last. And though he did have lingering feelings for her, just as she'd accused the night before, they weren't the kind of emotions that had the potential to rule his life, and he wasn't about to let her close enough to hurt him again. He needed to stop being a defensive jerk and remember that, despite the bitter break-up, they'd once been the closest of friends.

"Sure, but I need to finish up a couple of things first. Can you wait ten minutes?"

She nodded, though she still looked wary of his mood change. "Yeah. I need to wrap with the camera crew myself."

He nodded, then headed to the hauler. He quickly completed his breakdown routine and shut down his laptop.

Still, by the time he was finished Lizzie had settled into one of the director's chairs outside the hauler and a new crowd of autograph-seeking guys had gathered, as well as a man in a dark, intricately pressed suit. "Thanks, everybody," she said, rising from her chair and moving toward Dane.

With her gaze intent on his, Dane found pride swelling in his chest. Here was the simple girl he'd known so many years before, holding a crowd of seen-it-all race crew members in the palm of her hand.

As the crowd dispersed, Lizzie nodded toward the guy in the suit. "This is my driver, Vince Malleta. Vince, this is Dane Guthrie."

Dane shook hands with the other man, who, though shorter, was broader and heavily muscled. He looked more like a bodyguard than a driver, but he supposed Lizzie needed the former as much as the latter.

"He travels with me," she continued. "Is that okay?"

"Sure, but I've got a rental car in the parking lot," he said lamely.

Her lips lifted in an inviting smile, the one that had sold millions of CDs. "Don't worry. I'll arrange to have it returned to your hotel. Where are you staying?"

"The Waveview."

Her smile turned speculative. "No kidding? Me, too."

SHE SHOULDN'T HAVE shown off with the limo and driver thing.

The convenience of Vince and the luxury of a classy car were things she took for granted when she was traveling. There'd been a time when she'd been in awe; now it was normal.

She'd even pushed her power play by calling the hotel, who'd been only too happy to send a valet to the track to transfer Dane's car. That kind of show was something she'd outgrown many years before. Something she'd done to get people she wanted to impress to like her. She'd quickly learned that people she treated with kindness and respect generally liked her, and anybody swayed by the flash probably wouldn't wind up as a true friend anyway.

Was it because she was with her teenage lover that she reverted to adolescent behavior, or was she simply trying to show off for the grown man he'd become?

Either way, her behavior was embarrassing.

"Quite a coincidence that we're staying in the same hotel," she said as she sipped chardonnay across the table from Dane.

"We're sure not in the same room."

She choked. "No, I guess we're not." And yet the idea didn't bother her so much as seem unlikely.

"I mean, the same *kind* of room," Dane corrected, lifting his beer bottle. "I'm in a regular room with a king bed. You're probably in the presidential suite."

She was, actually, but she couldn't dismiss the idea of them in the same room, bringing back the memory of a low-rent hotel, on the edge of Florence, South Carolina, where they'd both grown up. The first night of intimacy for them both.

She'd loved him before that night and even more afterward. Why hadn't she been willing to fight for them?

But it seemed forays into the past were inevitable with Dane.

Even the restaurant/bar where they now sat was the kind of place they'd gone to in the old days. It was casual, crowded and beachside. After a quick conversation with Vince, the restaurant manager had been happy to give her and Dane a small table on a darkened corner of the deck so that she'd attract the least amount of attention.

Though with the biggest race of the season just over

a week away, she supposed people were more pumped about racing than music. It was oddly nice to be thought of as merely the opening act.

"Sorry I was rude before," Dane said, meeting her gaze and sending a jolt of desire through her as if minutes instead of years had passed since they'd been a couple. "There's a lot of pressure on my team, and I guess I'm not handling it very well."

"It's okay. I get the same way on tour."

"How do you deal with it?"

"I run on the treadmill until the frustration passes."

"You obviously run a lot, then."

"I do, in fact. Touring isn't as glamorous as you might—" She stopped and considered him. "Hang on. How do you know I run a lot?"

"You still have the best legs I've ever seen."

She blinked. A compliment and an apology in the space of five minutes? Despite his tendency toward wariness, Dane could be charming when he wanted. She'd forgotten just how much. "Thank you."

He leaned back, shaking his head. "I'm not sure why I seem to blurt out inappropriate things around you."

"Maybe I make you nervous."

His vivid green eyes seemed to burn into hers. "Maybe you do."

CHAPTER FOUR

SMILING SLIGHTLY, Lizzie held Dane's gaze. "Compliments aren't inappropriate, you know."

"I'm sure your boyfriend wouldn't agree."

"I don't have a boyfriend."

He paused with his beer bottle halfway to his mouth. "Why not?"

"*That's* an inappropriate question."

"Are all the men in Nashville blind?" he asked, ignoring her. "Hell, every man in the country?"

"I'm busy with other things besides romance." She raised her eyebrows. "Aren't you?"

"Sure, but I'm…"

"A man?"

"No. Well, yeah, but that wasn't what I was going to say."

"Then what?"

"I'm not you, and you should have a busy love life. You should be with someone like James Allenton."

No, she shouldn't. Hot? Yes. Self-absorbed egomaniac? Definitely. "I told you that was a publicity stunt and definitely not my idea." Watching him carefully, she sipped her wine. "But, I'm curious…how did you know about us?"

Obviously he figured he couldn't bluff his way out of the knowledge a second time. "I was in line at the grocery store, and there you were, with him, on the cover of some magazine." He narrowed his eyes. "I don't follow your love life like some obsessed fan."

"Oh, right." She nodded. "You're not a fan at all."

He shrugged. "I like to hear you sing."

His blasé answer sparked her competitive spirit. "Do you like my legs or my voice better?"

"I have to choose?"

She laughed and leaned back, crossing her legs. She liked knowing for certain that the chemistry wasn't one-sided. Whether he realized it or not, Dane was letting down his guard with her. "I work hard to keep both of them in shape, so, no, you don't have to choose."

"I guess I shouldn't have made you choose all those years ago."

"It hurt." She paused, then added, "And ticked me off."

"You hurt me, too." He turned his head toward the ocean, its relentless and powerful waves crashing on the sandy shore. "It's strange seeing you again. I thought that part of my life was over."

"Me, too," she admitted, mirroring his melancholy tone and studying his profile. The seaside breeze stirred the silky waves of dark brown hair that he'd once cut short to battle the curls.

His tanned and muscular forearms, resting on the table, spoke of the physical aspect of his profession. James Allenton, even with all his outward perfection, left her cold and bored. Dane's strength, passion and even his defensiveness drew her like a magnet.

The unexpected attraction that had sparked from the ashes of a hurtful past burned brighter with each moment they spent together. Lizzie wasn't sure if being with him was wise, but she couldn't seem to stop herself.

"I lied before," he said. "I am a fan. I've followed your career with great interest." He turned his head suddenly, smiling in such a disarming way, her breath caught. "Damned if you haven't made something of all that strumming and muttering."

Even as the warmth of his tone spread through her, his words landed. "Strumming and muttering?" she commented sharply. "Is that anything like your tinkering and fiddling?"

"Exactly like that," he said, nodding. "We both did what we wanted, Lizzie. We made our dreams come true."

"Which we wouldn't have done if we'd stayed together, is that what you're saying?"

"I am."

Somehow that seemed sad, not triumphant. "Maybe we could have done both."

"How do you mean?"

"Had successful careers and a happy family."

He shook his head. "No, we couldn't have."

His resignation bothered her in a way she couldn't completely explain. Why did they have to choose? Why was one not right with the other? "So you've stayed single to focus on your career?"

"How do you know I'm single?"

"I asked."

He should appreciate the candid answer. At least she hoped so.

She'd asked him out to mend fences and set the past aside. To be able to move beyond the regrets nagging her.

But with desire laying thick in the air, an impulse prodded her. Would a fling with an old love jolt her from the speculation of what might have been? Would a journey into the past answer her questions about the future?

There had to be more to life than recording and touring, interviews and fake relationships for the sake of publicity.

She wanted to be challenged and inspired again. She wanted to know if life could mean more than work and lonely nights—even those nights when she was surrounded by thousands of people.

Deep down, she longed for someone to share her success with. Given Dane's resentment of their breakup, she didn't see how that man could be him.

But, for now, he was just what she needed.

When he continued to stare at her, surprise evident in his eyes, she said, "I guess no irate girlfriend is going to charge out here, demanding to know why you're having a drink with a former lover."

"No. Why did you ask about me?"

"I don't have grocery store magazine racks to tell me what you're doing."

"Don't be obtuse, Lizzie. I meant, why do you care enough to ask about me?"

She glanced at the ocean before she spoke, hoping the sight would calm her. So many times lately she'd longed for the closeness of the sea. She felt certain her life wouldn't be so solitary and unsettled if she had the sand and brine to console her. Unfortunately, her stomach only rolled like the waves.

Forcing her gaze back to his, she asked, "Have you heard my new single? 'Long Gone'?"

He seemed confused by the change of subject. "Sure."

"It's about us."

He took a long pull of his beer. Stalling? Going over the lyrics in his mind?

If so, what did he think about the forlorn story of a woman who's reached the top, only to see her first love again and lament the wasted years they'd spent apart? To wish they could reconcile but have no idea how to overcome the pain of the past?

"The song's about regret," he said finally.

"Yes."

His hand tightened on his beer bottle until the knuckles turned white. "You regret leaving me?"

"In some ways."

"But everything in your life was wonderful after you left."

"Not everything."

Rising, she turned her back on him and stood at the wooden railing surrounding the deck. The moon was reflected in the water like a mirror. One she didn't want to look into.

She wasn't sure why she'd told him about the song; she hadn't planned to.

But he'd let down his guard a bit, so she knew she had to take the same leap. She didn't like looking back at their breakup and wondering what might have been. She didn't like fearing she'd traded lifelong love for crystal trophies and platinum CDs. Was she really that shallow and ambitious?

"You did the right thing," he said quietly from behind her.

"Did I? I suppose my manager and agent think so."

"And your fans." He stood next to her, leaning against the railing. "Think of all the people who love your music, the millions you've entertained and touched over the years. That stands a whole lot taller than a teenage affair."

She met his gaze. "Does it? You're content with trophies and race wins?"

He moved his palm over the back of her hand, sliding his fingers between hers and squeezing. "That's what I've got. And I'm proud of each one of those accomplishments."

She looked down at their joined hands. Holding his hand used to make her blush. And, later, when their relationship deepened, he'd slide his thumb back and forth along her wrist just before a performance to calm her.

She'd never told him his presence alone was enough to make everything right.

She shook her head to clear it. Half a glass of wine and she'd turned melancholy. "That's very practical."

"You expect something else from me?"

"No way." She smiled. "Remember the first time I sang the national anthem at that old track on the beach. It wasn't even NASCAR sanctioned and you were rewiring the PA system right up until the last minute?"

"I should've charged that yahoo promoter two hundred bucks for the job."

"Since he didn't even have the money for the race purse, I bet his check would've bounced."

Dane nodded. "We literally chased him from the track."

"Instead of hoes and pitchforks, it was wrenches and tire irons. A crew chief/driver mob."

"Don't forget the fans tossing popcorn and chips." His gaze roved her face. "And you were still the star of the night."

She angled her body toward him. "Funny, I thought you were."

They stood so close, their chests nearly brushed. Air backed up in her lungs like a sputtering engine and made breathing difficult. She could feel his rapid pulse against her skin. The scent of salty air brought the past back so vividly, she was almost sure she could reach out and hold it in her hand.

Leaning toward her, Dane angled his head.

"Excuse me, Ms. Lancaster," Vince said, extending a cell phone. "It's Ronnie. He says it's urgent."

Dane stepped back, and Lizzie vowed to strangle her manager.

"You'll never guess who's going to be at qualifying tomorrow," Ronnie said in a rush the moment she put the phone to her ear.

She barely resisted the urge to sigh. Weren't you supposed to be able to work less once you were successful? "Who?"

"Joe Calponi."

"Who?" she repeated as Dane returned to his seat at the table, and she felt the distance between them widen more than just physically.

"He's a movie producer, darling," Ronnie said.

Ronnie had been trying to push her into the Hollywood scene for nearly a year, and she always had the same argument to every lame project he proposed. "I'm not an actress. I'm a singer."

"Nobody expects an Academy Award," Ronnie continued. "At least not for acting. But…" He paused dramatically. Ronnie certainly knew the art of pacing a story. "Joe does have several."

"Yay for him. How does this involve me?"

"Joe loves 'Long Gone' like his firstborn child, and he wants to use it in his next movie. This is the real deal, sweetie. Your entree into the movie industry. Who knows, we might even spend next spring walking the red carpet."

Lizzie sincerely hoped the firstborn child reference could be laid at Ronnie's dramatic feet, but given the odd meetings she'd had with movie producers over the years, she couldn't be entirely sure.

She was a simple girl from South Carolina, who loved to sing. She happened to be good at it. Surely she didn't need more than that.

But an ambitious entertainer lived inside her. A girl who'd longed for the spotlight and to be somebody important.

One of her songs in an award-winning producer's movie? Wow. Wasn't that the opportunity of a lifetime? She had to be absolutely out of her mind not to be tempted.

"Can you set up a meeting tomorrow?" she asked.

"Already have, darling. Be ready to leave by ten in the morning. I even found a makeup artist to fix you up. He'll be there at eight-thirty."

A makeup artist? She wasn't going on stage. "I don't need—"

"Get some rest, beautiful."

She didn't bother to say anything to the dead air and instead pressed the disconnect button, then handed the phone to the silently waiting Vince.

"It seems I have an appointment at the track tomorrow," she said as she returned to her seat across from Dane. To even mention the word Oscars seemed pretentious, so she didn't.

Dane nodded. "I have to be at the track early, too. Maybe we should go."

She glanced at her watch. "It's only eleven."

"I have notes to go over." He signaled for the waiter, who laid the check next to him.

Lizzie laid her hand over Dane's. "I invited you. Let me take care of the bill."

"I've got it."

Nothing in his tone betrayed anything but politeness, but she sensed a change regardless. As they walked to the limo, she considered it was probably rude to take a call from her manager while on a date, but before she could apologize, he asked about her parents and sisters.

Chatting about people they'd both known growing up, they rode in the limo toward the hotel, sitting next to each other, but not touching. The way old acquaintances would act. Perfectly normal and yet something was different. She didn't bring up the near kiss and even wondered if she'd mistaken his intentions before the call had interrupted them.

As they pulled up to the hotel portico, she waited for Vince to open her door, but Dane had already climbed out and had extended his hand for hers before her driver could get there.

"I'll make sure she gets to her room," Dane said to Vince.

Vince looked to her for confirmation, and she nodded, thanking him for taking such good care of them and wishing him good-night.

As they rode in the elevator to the top floor, Dane stood with his hands clasped behind his back, watching the numbered lights illuminate in succession. He was silent, seemingly deep in thought.

"Are you okay?" she asked when the doors opened and they walked into the hall.

"Sure."

First date nerves jangled in her stomach. Would he try to kiss her? Were his thoughts on her or tomorrow's qualifying? Could this even be considered a date?

The Dane she'd known wouldn't miss an opportunity to touch her—ever. But then they'd had to sneak kisses between races and voice lessons and around teachers and parents. Plus, she didn't know him anymore, did she? They'd caught up on the basics and talked out the mistakes of the past, but what did they really have?

It wasn't often she was so unsure of herself, and she found she didn't like the sensation one little bit.

She opened the door and stepped across the threshold. "You want to—"

"So, a big movie deal is in the works?" he asked abruptly, leaning against the door frame.

Her gaze jumped to him. His tone wasn't so much a question as a challenge.

"I wear earplugs at the track, but nowhere else," he said, raising his eyebrows. "Ronnie's voice carries when he's excited."

"It's all speculative," she countered, relieved this was what had him so deep in thought. "If you knew how many times—"

"It's where you belong. I belong at the track, and you belong with the stars."

Maybe their lives were worlds apart. But she didn't want them to be. And she sensed part of him didn't, either.

The longing between them was as tangible as the walls, floors and ceiling surrounding them.

She'd once known him like her own hand. They'd shared everything—hopes, dreams, and every emotion imaginable. But she wasn't sure how to reach the man who'd been the boy she loved.

"Yes, we have different jobs," she said. "But that's all they are—jobs. Prosecutors and defense attorneys occupy the same courthouse. Fans of opposing drivers live in the same home. Cats and dogs get along…sometimes."

The last drew a reluctant smile from his lips.

"And yet you seemed determined to point out our differences." She looked into his eyes. "Why is that? Why are you so determined to keep your distance from me?"

"We may be worlds apart, Lizzie, but that doesn't mean I don't want you anyway."

Then he wrapped his arm around her waist, pulled her against his chest and kissed her.

CHAPTER FIVE

SHE'D WRITTEN a song about him.

That knowledge spread a warmth through Dane's chest he hadn't felt in fourteen years. If it wasn't a sad, hopeless song, he might even be elated.

As his mouth moved over hers and she wrapped her arms around his neck, he closed his eyes, eager to absorb every sensation, barely believing he was touching her again.

When they separated, her breathing had quickened, and her eyes had darkened to a deep ocean blue, filled with desire. "I'm not doing such a great job of keeping my distance," he said huskily.

Her gaze dropped to his lips. "You won't hear me complain."

Cupping her cheek, he kissed her again, pouring all the pain, frustration and loneliness he'd felt ever since she'd left him for her life in Nashville. Why had he held on to his bitterness for so long when he could have had this—her touch, her warm, exotic scent twisting around him, binding them together?

"I need to go," he said when he pulled back.

She glanced behind her as if she was considering inviting him into her room, which he both hoped she'd do and hoped she'd resist.

He was weak and wanted her desperately, but the saner side of him knew they couldn't go from old lovers, to distant strangers to lovers again in the space of twenty-four hours. They both needed to take a long step backward and figure out what they were doing, what this chemistry between them meant.

"I guess so." She drew her arms from around his neck and moved away. "Thanks for the drink."

"Anytime. Will I see you tomorrow?"

"Yeah. I'll come by the hauler when I can."

"Let me know how the meeting goes, okay?" He couldn't resist one last stroke of his hand against her silky cheek. "My Lizzie going Hollywood. Pretty amazing."

MY LIZZIE?

What delusional, irrational, reckless part of him had driven him to say that?

The next morning as he drove himself and several of his crew members to the track, Dane barely saw the road in front of him, since he was too busy reliving the startled look in Lizzie's eyes the night before.

A woman like her was no man's possession. And, in some ways, she belonged to everybody *but* him.

He was just another fan. The only unique thing about him was that he was a fan who'd known her before she'd become a superstar.

And you kissed her like you were in fear of expressing your last breathing seconds on the planet.

Ridiculously, he wondered how many times James Allenton had done the same. Though she claimed their relationship was a publicity stunt—which was the most un-Lizzie thing he'd ever heard of—he knew no sane man could be within touching distance of that stunning face for long and not want to lay his hands on her.

"Is something wrong with the car, chief?"

The question had been asked by one of the mechanics in the backseat.

"No," Dane said shortly, then sipped his coffee and hoped that would be the end of the inquiries. No way could he admit his mind had been anywhere but on racing.

"You seem a little…edgy," the mechanic said.

Dane directed his gaze to the rearview mirror. "Can you think of a better reason to be edgy than qualifying at Daytona?"

"No, I guess not."

Silence fell. Dane's mind went back to the publicity stunt.

The Lizzie he knew was determined, focused and stubborn as hell. Who had talked her into pretending she and Allenton were an item? How? Was this the kind of thing she did to sell more CDs?

He could believe such a scheme of her slick manager, but not her. Lizzie's heart was in the music, the songs she wrote to express herself and share with anyone who'd ever felt the same way.

And she'd written a song about him.

He was honored and shocked and confused. The attraction they'd always shared hadn't diminished, even after all the time spent apart, and yet he couldn't trust that desire. His heart wasn't healed from the last time she'd broken it.

Had he had a part in his own destruction?

Absolutely.

But what practical man in his right mind would go there again?

As the granddaddy track loomed in the distance, Dane took a moment to appreciate its awesome size and significance in history before he turned down a side road to avoid the main entrance and get to the infield more quickly.

Fans, who certainly knew as many back roads as the teams, were already lined up, waving signs and hoping to catch a glimpse of their favorite driver. Their devotion was a marvel, but only served to remind Dane of the pressures of the tasks ahead.

He parked the rental car in one of the infield lots, then he and his guys headed toward the garage.

As the familiar smells of rubber, fuel and grilled meats hit him, his focus finally snapped into place. His job had to take priority now. Lizzie, and all the complications she presented, would be there after qualifying.

Even though only the two cars starting on the front row would be determined that afternoon, the speeds would establish which of the two duel races they'd run in on Thursday, and those races would set the field for the all-important season-opening event.

Through the morning preparation, Dane kept his thoughts on the checklist and combing the car for any missed detail or potential problem. When Kelsey arrived, he encouraged the team to joke with her and keep her calm.

She was a professional and may not need the hand-holding, but there was no way she wasn't nervous and somewhat intimidated by the people who'd gone through this routine year after year. This was her first qualifying session in a stock car, and he knew she wanted to impress her colleagues.

When it was their turn to make the two-lap run, he watched from the top of the hauler as the team's safety director handed over her helmet and secured her in the car.

"You've got this," Dane said to Kelsey into the radio. "Just hit your marks. You'll be fine."

"What if I forget to breathe?"

"I'll remind you."

She apparently did remember to breathe, because she didn't pass out and instead ran a blistering lap that put her in sixth. By the time the afternoon session wound down and everyone had taken their turn, she'd qualified tenth.

While she smiled her way through the media interviews, Dane and the rest of the team packed up the equipment. Everyone was optimistic about their chances in the race, and after the humiliating next-to-last-place finish the night before, they could all use the boost.

But during a team meeting, Dane's cell phone rang with lousy news from the shop back in Mooresville. The crew there was having problems with the cars they were preparing for California and Vegas. The seven-post's testing results were way off what they'd expected, and they wanted to know if he could come back for a day or two and talk about how to handle the situation.

After qualifying, the track would be closed for two days, so most team members, drivers, owners, fans, families—pretty much everybody—were headed to the beach, the local short tracks or the theme parks around Orlando for a little R&R.

Apparently some crew chiefs, like him, would continue to work.

After talking to owner Jim Latimer, he called the shop and assured them he'd be back that night. They'd have nearly two full days to work through the problems for the upcoming weeks. Though Daytona was the grand-prize race for the season, there were thirty-five other trophies up for grabs. Dane couldn't take the chance on victoriously leaving Florida but sucking wind everywhere else.

He just finished exchanging messages with Jim's pilot, arranging to meet at the airport ASAP when Lizzie texted him to let him know she was on her way to see him.

His heart gave an excited leap, even though his no-nonsense nature tried to talk him down from the clouds. It was laughable to think he'd hold her interest for long. And while he did, would he continue to give in to the temptation to see her every second he could? Continue to say and think ridiculous things like *my Lizzie?*

He was certain he would. Every man had a weakness. And Lizzie was definitely his.

The only thing putting distance between them were circumstances beyond his control. It seemed fate would be practical when he couldn't.

In the middle of packing his laptop, the door opened and Gavin, the hauler driver, stuck his head around the edge. "You've got a visitor. She's, uh…outside, signing autographs."

"Send her back."

Gavin's eyebrows rose almost as high as his thinning hairline. "You *know* Lizzie Lancaster?"

"Send her back now."

"You bet."

"Thank you so much, Gavin," he heard Lizzie say from the hall moments later. "This is just what I needed."

"Can I get you anything else, Ms. Lancaster?" Gavin asked, his tone reverent.

"The water's great, really."

Dane stopped fastening the buckles on his bag for the simple pleasure of watching her walk into the room. Today's ensemble might be titled "Country Music Star at Leisure." She wore a flouncy, expensive-looking pale green shirt, dark jeans that hugged her lean curves and high-heeled brown shoes. Her hair was curled around her face and streamed past her shoulders like flame-colored silk. Triumph and pleasure rode high in her eyes, making her beauty all the more spectacular.

Gavin pulled the door closed behind her and, somehow, Dane found his voice. "Promise me you won't visit on race day."

"Why in the world not?"

"My team will be too busy drooling to get any work done." He took her hand and drew her to the sofa, then reluctantly let her go and leaned back against the desk nearby. "So?"

"Well, it looks I'm going to the movies."

"I'm guessing it won't be to see the latest block-buster adventure."

"I think Joe Calponi is known more for his dramas." When he nodded, she added, "And his four Oscars."

"Right. That historical thing a few years back."

She nodded. "*The French Widower's Mistress.* The film won several big awards, including Best Song, plus it apparently broke every box-office record in the country. Now it seems Joe's decided to move away from the war-torn forties and come south." Her gaze met Dane's, and he finally saw the tension beneath the happiness. "For once, Ronnie didn't exaggerate. The producer loves 'Long Gone' and definitely wants to use it in his new film."

He rose, intending to embrace her. It was so amazing. Lizzie's song in a—

Lizzie's song about them. About regret and sorrow. The one that ends with the old lovers seeing each other again, but are too wounded and stubborn to admit they still care for each other and part, never reconciling their feelings.

"I've agreed," she added, standing when he remained silent. "The song wasn't written for the movie, which is already in production, so I couldn't actually win an award, of course. Not that I ever would anyway. But with Joe's respect in the industry, the song will get lots of exposure. It'll be included in the movie soundtrack. Ronnie even has this delusional idea that I might get invited to sing at the ceremony next year. I can't imagine that, but, well, the possibility's there." She bit her lip and clenched her fists by her sides. "Dammit, Dane, say something."

Immediately, he reached out and pulled her into his arms. "It's great," he assured her, even though he felt sick inside. He kissed her cheek. "Amazing. Congratulations."

"Except that our story will be exposed."

"Nobody has to know it's about us."

"But we'll know. *You'll* know." She leaned back, her gaze searching his. "I wrote the song when I was sad, and I really wasn't sure I wanted to include it on the CD, but Ronnie talked me into it. He said the emotions were too powerful not to share." She rolled her eyes as if she, too, thought Ronnie would say anything to sell a song.

"It's fine," he said automatically, though the idea of something so personal being downloaded on MP3 players by the millions gave his pulse a bad jolt.

"I never dreamed I'd see you again and have to explain." She paced away from him. "Well, maybe unconsciously I did. Maybe that's why I wrote it in the first place." She waved her hand as if dismissing the idea. "I could rewrite the ending, I guess."

His heart was still beating a little too fast for him to get a handle on what the song and the movie might mean. "Why would you do that?"

"Because we've already admitted our regrets. And we sure won't walk away from each other without talking about our feelings."

"We won't?"

Stopping, she faced him with her eyes narrowed. "At least *I* won't. I assume from the soul-stirring kisses of last night that you won't claim we're just old pals who happen to be in the same place at the same time."

"I'm not big on talking about my feelings."

"Sure you aren't. Testosterone is a natural blocker." She moved toward him, stopping when they were bare inches apart. She drew her index finger down the center of his chest. "That excuse won't save you from me, however."

"I'm fine with the song. Really," he added, his voice going up a stressful octave that no member of his team or any other in the garage would believe he was capable of. "It's great. I really like it."

"Do you really?" she asked, her sarcasm clear.

"Sure." He nodded for emphasis. His pulse raced with the need to escape her touch, the attraction between them and the scary emotions she inspired. His broken love for her had devastated him to the point that he'd never been able to commit to another woman. It never even occurred to him that he'd one day end up married, happy and settled. He always looked to the next race, the next season and kept his involvement with women limited to the purely temporary variety.

Lizzie couldn't change all that with a kiss and a song.

Could she?

"You're not seriously going to pretend you don't want me?" she demanded.

"Of course I want you."

"Then what's the problem?"

"I have to go home."

"Oh, that's a really lame excuse. You don't honestly expect me to believe…"

She trailed off when he pulled his phone from his pocket and showed her the message from the pilot. "But I thought we could spend some time at the beach. Maybe talk about last night."

He recovered enough sense to remember that his time with Lizzie was limited. When she made her movie debut, he'd be a distant memory. But one he wanted her to at least remember warmly.

"I'd like that, too," he said. As long as they could focus on the kissing and skip the painful soul-baring. He clasped her hands in his. "There are urgent problems at the race shop I have to take care of. I'll be back Wednesday. How about we have dinner that night?"

"Don't you have a race to call on Thursday?"

He shrugged. "I probably won't sleep the night before anyway. I might as well not sleep with you."

She pressed her lips together, obviously to hold back her laughter. "What girl could resist such a charming invitation?"

CHAPTER SIX

LIZZIE RECLINED on the balcony of her beachside hotel with a sigh.

She'd spent the morning with her guitar, working on a new song. With "Long Gone" fresh on her mind, and the memory of yesterday's blazing hot goodbye kiss from Dane to inspire her, she hoped she'd penned another hit.

She often wrote about the ups and downs of her relationships. The honesty in her inability to find love was something she was sure her fans responded to, because everybody went through the same thing at some point in their life. But she couldn't remember the last time a specific man had inspired one song, much less two.

Usually her lyrics and the emotions that inspired them were more general and euphemistic. Then again every romantic relationship she'd ever gone through stemmed, one way or another, from Dane.

So what the devil was she doing, sitting and staring at the ocean while he was five hundred miles away? Didn't she have a plane and a rare few days of free time? Even the NCV crew had shut down to enjoy the beach.

If Dane had to be home in North Carolina, then she could be there, too.

She sneaked away with Vince and one small suit-case. Feeling oddly rebellious and free as she rode in the rental car from the airport to the race shop, she realized it had been years since she'd been on her own. She usually had a schedule and a team of people to do everything from brush her hair to order her dinner.

Did she really need all that? When had she started having her makeup professionally done even when she was simply going to a meeting? When had life become so complicated and sheltered, but markedly unfulfilled?

Was being around Dane again reminding her of simpler times or was she finally waking up to realize she'd allowed her life to be choreographed instead of lived?

By the time Vince pulled the car into the parking lot at PDQ Racing, it was nearly three o'clock. She walked into the lobby with Vince hovering just behind her and approached the receptionist desk and the young blonde woman manning it. "Hi, I'd like to see Dane Guthrie, please."

"I'm sorry. He's—" the receptionist stopped, her eyes widening. "Has anybody ever told you that you look just like Lizzie Lancaster?"

Lizzie smiled. "All the time."

The receptionist's fair skin flushed. "You're her, aren't you?"

"I am. What's your name?"

"Tina Houston."

"Nice to meet you, Tina. Is there any way you could send me back to Dane's office without announcing me—if he's not busy, that is? We're old friends, and I wanted to surprise him."

"You know Mr. Guthrie?" she asked, her eyes wide as saucers. "I mean, he knows *you?*"

Were she and Dane such opposites that it seemed impossible they were friends? "We know each other, yes. Could I…?" Lizzie trailed off and pointed at the door just beyond the receptionist station marked Private.

"Oh, sure." Tina rose. "I'd be glad to take you back to Mr. Guthrie's office, only he's not there." She angled her head. "Could you wait for him maybe?"

Deflated, Lizzie blinked. "Where is he?"

"He and Mr. Ballentine—he's one of our engineers—went down to Maudie's for a late lunch." She glanced at her watch. "They should be back in half an hour or so. I could get you some tea or coffee while you wait."

This is what she got for not calling first. Despite her earlier thoughts about not needing a team of people around her all the time, the slightly spoiled star deep inside her was annoyed. "What's Maudie's?"

"It's a diner just down the road. Everybody from the shops eats there."

"Could you give me directions? I could still surprise him."

"Sure." She leaned over her desk and scribbled a map and brief directions, then handed the piece of paper to Lizzie. "Is James Allenton just as hot in person?" she asked in a breathless rush.

Lizzie grinned. "Definitely." She waved the note. "Thanks."

The ride to the restaurant took less than ten minutes, and Lizzie entered with the realization that Tina had described it perfectly. Maudie's was a diner straight out of the 1950s. Chrome trim decorated the bar stools and countertops, while red vinyl booths stood out against the black-and-white checkered floor. Photographs of NASCAR drivers both modern and past were scattered over the baby blue walls.

And, naturally, hanging over the bar was a pink neon sign, proclaiming Maudie's Down Home Diner.

Though late for lunch, the place was packed with men in dark blue mechanic's uniforms sporting various logos from race teams. Several people looked in her direction as she walked inside, but they all immediately went back to their meals or coffee cups.

She sensed Vince moving closer, as they were both used to her being recognized and often surrounded before she could blink.

Being ignored was a weird experience.

"Can I help you?"

Lizzie headed toward the source of the voice—a tiny redhead, wiping the long bar with a white cloth, her wavy ponytail bouncing as she moved. "I'm looking for Dane Guthrie. Do you know him?"

"Sure. He's right over there," the woman said, pointing to a booth in the back corner, where Dane was deep into an apparently serious conversation with a man Lizzie didn't recognize. "I'm Sheila, by the way. This is my place."

Lizzie shook her hand, finding the other woman's palm rough and her grip firm. This was a woman who took charge. "Not Maudie?"

"She was the original owner."

"Oh. I'm Lizzie, nice to meet you."

She had no idea why she hadn't given her last name. Some instinct that neither this woman nor her patrons would give two hangs about who she was and how many CDs she'd sold, told her that first names were enough.

"Dane's a nice guy," Sheila continued. "Have you known him long?"

"We went to high school together."

Speculation flashed in her warm brown eyes. "No kidding." Her gaze moved to a point over Lizzie's shoulder. "Hey, I'm Sheila."

Lizzie glanced back at Vince. She supposed it had been rude not to introduce him, but his silent hovering was as normal as knowing all her limbs were in working order. "This is Vince. My…companion."

"Okay." If she found Vince's silence, or Lizzie's description of his role odd, she didn't point it out. "I'll send your waitress over to take your order when she's free."

"I'm fine. Vince would probably like a cup of coffee, though." Lizzie patted the bar stool in front of her. "Have a seat, Vince. Sheila doesn't look like she'd bite."

"Not hard anyway," Sheila returned.

Vince stood rooted in place, glancing from Lizzie to Sheila, then the table in the corner where Dane sat as if wondering if the proposed arrangement suited him. Finally, he nodded and slid onto the stool.

Many women had found Vince's Italian looks and intensity irresistible. His reluctance to speak was a minor flaw most people wouldn't point out to his beefy frame and dark, dangerous eyes.

"I'll be back in a few minutes," Lizzie said, turning away.

"You've got a nice voice," Sheila said.

Lizzie glanced over her shoulder. Oh, yeah. Sheila was definitely nobody's fool. "Thanks." Then, with a roll of her shoulders, she headed toward the reason she'd crossed two and a half states in the hope of connecting with a past she'd turned her back on long ago.

DANE PAUSED with a forkful of mashed potatoes halfway to his mouth.

Lizzie?

He blinked, certain he was hallucinating. But Lizzie, dressed in faded jeans, a white shirt and a brown suede jacket, was still moving toward him.

Even though Floyd was in the middle of a sentence, Dane rose and faced Lizzie. "What are you doing here?"

Her deep blue eyes flickered with censure, but she slid her arms lightly around his waist and kissed his cheek. "I heard about Sheila's great food and decided to stop by."

"That's…nice," he said, slowly realizing the impact of what she'd done. She'd come to Mooresville to see *him.* He'd left, and she'd come after him as he'd fantasized doing himself thousands of times before. If he'd given in to any of those impulses, would she have been as elated as he was now?

Could he have changed everything simply by going after her all those years ago? Could he change the ending of the song?

He shook his head. "I'm just…"

"Surprised? Suspicious?" Her gaze met his, and his pulse leapt. "Thrilled?"

"Happy," he said simply, surprised at the sentiment and the admission.

The clang of silverware from a nearby table finally jolted him from his shock and reminded him where he was. "Lizzie, this is Floyd Ballentine, one of the engineers at PDQ. Floyd, Lizzie Lancaster."

Before the first syllables were out of Dane's mouth, Floyd had risen and was nervously wringing his hands in front of him. "I'm a big fan. We listen to your songs all the time at the shop."

Lizzie smiled broadly at Floyd. "That's so nice. Thank you." She directed her attention back to Dane. "You listen, too?"

"Oh, yeah," Floyd answered for him, pushing his glasses farther up on his nose. "Dane's usually the first one with your new CD. We load our favorite tracks on the shop MP3 player and listen while we work."

Lizzie raised her eyebrows. "No kidding."

What was Floyd talking about? He was a brilliant engineer, but not so sharp on certain details. He'd obviously overlooked the fact that Dane wasn't usually the first one to show up with Lizzie's new CD. He was *always* the first one.

But then he didn't want either of them to examine that reality too closely. "Have you eaten?" he asked Lizzie, urging her into the booth beside him. "Let me get you something." He raised his hand to signal for the waitress.

Lizzie tugged his arm down. Her eyes danced with familiar amusement. "I'll just share with you."

How many times had they done that because neither of them had the money for two plates? The memory brought a sharp ache to his chest. So long ago, and yet yesterday was sitting beside him.

Well aware they weren't even close to being alone, he shook his head. "I don't think so. I know how you can eat."

She swatted his shoulder. "That's completely untrue." Her gaze moved to Floyd, who was still staring at her as if a star had suddenly fallen from the sky, which, basically, it had. "I've interrupted your meeting. I just wanted to let you know I was here. Maybe we can meet for dinner later?"

Under the table, Dane gripped her hand tightly in his. No way was he letting her out of his sight. "We were wrapping things up."

"Except for the problem with the downforce on the California car, chief," Floyd said, and Dane could have cheerfully strangled him. "The seven-post data isn't pretty."

Lizzie squeezed Dane's hand, then she reached into her bag for her cell phone. "You guys go ahead. I'll check my messages. I left sort of…abruptly. My staff is probably climbing the walls by now."

The shocks just kept on coming.

She'd taken Vince and run away from her staff to be with him. Determined. Focused. Stubborn. *His* Lizzie.

What would happen if he was the thing she was focused on? What would happen if he returned her attention? If they set their careers aside and made each other a priority?

Would he finally find the future he'd given up on years ago?

"One question, though," she said, cocking her head. "What's a seven-post?"

Dane nodded at Floyd, who was clearly dying to answer. "We run a real car at a race track with computer probes attached in various places. Those probes measure every movement of the car—the springs, shocks, the steering input by the driver, the altitude of the vehicle front to rear and side to side. We can then take those actual measurements and plug them into a computer program that will download that data into a machine that has seven poles, or posts, connected to the car. Each post is hydraulically activated by the computer program to simulate exactly on the machine what the car goes through at speed on the race track.

"Then we can make changes to the car while it's on the machine, like change springs, shocks, sway bars, or even air pressure of the tires, like we would during a real practice session at the track and determine what effect each change has on the car. And we can do all of that without all of the cost involved and travel time of sending a crew halfway across the country to test at a real track."

Lizzie said nothing for a long moment. "You guys have fun with that," she commented finally. "I'll stick with my guitar."

What she could do with a guitar was way more of an art than the magic of a seven-post, but Dane dutifully discussed the problems with Floyd while trying to ignore the light tapping of Lizzie's fingers on her phone's keyboard.

She'd come after him.

She'd probably been offered a thousand glamorous

invitations with any number of important people, but she chose to be with him.

Truth be told, she'd always chosen him. Over all the cool football and baseball players in high school who'd chased her, she'd never wavered from her devotion to him. He'd been a quiet math geek who spent his weekends at the race track. She'd been the president of the drama and choral clubs. She'd directed every high school musical since her freshman year.

Everyone within ten miles of her knew she was a star in the making, but she'd told him she admired his determination and his easy grasp of Algebra. He'd tutored her every Wednesday at the library; he'd fallen in love after the first twenty minutes.

Just before graduation he'd issued his brash ultimatum that it had to be him or music. Fear and practicality had finally taken hold of his senses. He was headed to Charlotte to pursue his dreams in racing, and she had to go to Nashville to fulfill her own aspirations.

He was glad she'd chosen music. It was the right thing. Her destiny. His, too.

He'd been holding her back from going after her dreams. He'd been terrified of becoming her significant other sidekick and never realizing his own goals.

The sacrifice of parting had nearly killed him, but then that was no doubt his penitence for the shocked betrayal he'd put in her eyes.

He wasn't sure they could move beyond that maelstrom of betrayal, selfishness and sacrifice, but he knew he wanted to find out. If she was willing to come to him, he could make sure she stayed.

For however long he could hold her.

He finished his meeting with Floyd, paid the bill, then they all walked outside, waving at Sheila as they left.

There was an awkward moment on the sidewalk where Dane remembered he'd ridden to the diner in Floyd's car, and Lizzie had arrived separately. But Floyd discreetly moved several feet from him, while Vince fell silently into step behind Lizzie. "I'll start the car," he said, then melted away.

"I've got to go back to the shop for a while," Dane said to Lizzie with no small amount of regret. "Can I come get you around seven for dinner?"

"Sure." Giving him the name of her hotel, she stepped back. "I'll see you then."

He captured her hand in his before she could retreat further. "I'm sorry I have to work."

"No problem." She smiled. "Remember my patient cooperation when you're waiting for me backstage during a three-hour show."

Though he nodded, he knew her interest in him would be history by the time she went back on tour. "I should have invited you to come back here with me. I didn't think—"

She laid her finger over his lips before he could finish and admit it had never occurred to him that she'd want to. He couldn't reasonably expect her to hang around Mooresville while he worked from dawn to well past dusk.

"I'm here now," she said softly. "And we can make up for lost time."

CHAPTER SEVEN

FOR THE NEXT TWO DAYS, Lizzie stayed in an anonymous, moderately priced chain hotel—the same type race fans no doubt flooded to every time there was a race in the Charlotte area for its proximity to both the lake and the race shops.

There was no room service, valet or concierge. She walked next door to the Waffle House for breakfast; she ate dinner with Dane. On Tuesday morning, she rented a pontoon boat and floated aimlessly around Lake Norman with Vince as the pilot. That afternoon, she got a tour of the race shop and met the dedicated people at PDQ, many of whom rarely had the opportunity to see their hard work actually pay off in a live race.

Other than the singular complaint from Vince that he'd resorted to watching professional pool on the sports channels during the hours she retreated to her room composing, it was paradise.

By the time Wednesday afternoon rolled around, and Vince was driving her to PDQ to pick up Dane for the short journey to the airport, she'd written three more songs and felt more relaxed and in control of her destiny than she had in years.

Froufrou spas were way overrated.

As Vince pulled the car up to the back entrance of the shop, Floyd was waiting. She handed him the basket she'd made that morning, which was filled with autographed CDs, T-shirts, tickets to future concerts—everything Lizzie could think of to thank the PDQ staff for their warm welcome.

"You're a pretty special lady," Floyd said after a brief glance at the basket's contents.

Unexpectedly, tears flooded Lizzie's eyes.

Floyd hadn't commented on her songs, her voice, the awards she'd received or the sales numbers she'd collected. He appreciated her as a person. He thought she was nice and considerate.

What more could she wish for?

As she hugged Floyd, Dane strolled outside. "Well, well, well," he said, leaning back against the wall, crossing his arms over his broad chest. "One of my own team, going behind my back and trying to steal my woman."

His woman?

With a challenge and a question, Lizzie turned her gaze to Dane. They'd spent the last two nights sharing meals and memories. They'd also shared little more than a few kisses.

But still he held back.

He'd been a gracious and perfect gentleman, which she appreciated. He'd also been a confidant to all the frustration she'd been experiencing with her career and its responsibilities, which she needed. So, though their bond had strengthened, she was edgy, needy and anxious for more. She knew she had to be the one to move things forward. There was an odd barrier between them concerning Lizzie the Woman and Lizzie the Country Music Star.

She headed toward him, sliding her hand slowly up his chest to wrap around his neck. "You don't have to do much to make me all yours," she whispered in his ear.

As she felt his body jolt in shock, she smiled in satisfaction and stepped back, turning to Floyd. "I'll be watching closely this season. You guys better kick some butt."

Floyd puffed out his bony chest. "We will. Come back and see us."

"Count on it." She directed her attention to Dane, who hadn't moved from his position by the door. "Well, chief, are you ready to go back to Daytona?"

He pushed away from the wall and closed the distance between them in two easy strides. The intensity of his stare and the confident strength in the way he moved his body distracted her to the point that she had to nudge her legs to carry her toward the car as if they'd forgotten how to work.

As Vince held open the door, Dane assisted her inside the rented SUV, and they headed to the airport. By the time they were seated on her plane and airborne, she'd run through and discarded dozens of seduction scenarios.

She and Dane were running out of time. He had a race to run in a few days, then he'd be off to the next track…and the next. She had several charity events to do, then she was on to rehearsals for the spring tour, then the actual tour.

Their connection would be broken with distance if they didn't take their relationship to another level. She was sure of it.

"Nervous?"

She pulled her gaze from the clouds and sky out her window and glanced over at Dane, sitting beside her. "Why would I be nervous?"

"Don't know. But you are."

He reached out and folded her hand in his, sliding his thumb back and forth along the underside of her wrist.

And just like that, she fell in love with him all over again.

Without a word, with only the slightest of touches, she belonged to him—just as she always had.

Fear and delight fought against each other. He'd broken their bond with his ultimatum. Her heart had retreated, only showing itself in her music. Only popping out from behind her confidence when she was alone and quiet. Which is why she'd avoided being alone and quiet.

But the bond between her and Dane simply couldn't die. Time, distance, anger and doubt had driven them apart, and though circumstances had brought them back together, she knew she'd never really left at all.

She'd always been waiting for him to come after her.

"What's going on?" he asked, his deep green eyes concerned.

"Nothing. I'm just—" She stopped. Her feelings were the kind of thing she couldn't just drop casually into conversation. She had to find just the right words, and the importance of her emotions had the poet in her running for cover. "I'm nervous about singing the anthem on Sunday."

He scoffed.

"It's a hard song to sing."

"I bet you can handle it."

"Plus I have to sing it in front of about eight jillion people."

"Eight jillion, huh? Remind me to look that up in my math textbook."

His assurance in her abilities, and especially the casual way he spoke, reminded her that she didn't need fancy words. She'd lead with her heart. What else could she do? "Plus, *you* make me nervous."

"Me? How's that?"

She smiled. "You're my man. I'm trying to impress you."

He suddenly looked away. "About that…" His thumb moving against her wrist increased in speed. Now who was nervous? "I know I have no claim on you."

"Don't you?" She laid her fingers along his jaw, urging his face toward her. "You're my first love, Dane. Part of you will always belong to me."

His answer was to press his lips against hers. She felt his desire, but not his heart. He was still holding back.

She'd find a way to reach him. She had to. Her happiness, the final piece that would make her life complete was within her grasp. Running away again wasn't an option.

"Where do you want to eat?" he whispered against her cheek. "I promised you dinner when we got back, remember?"

She shifted her gaze directly to his. "How about room service?"

WEARING ONLY HIS JEANS and sipping from a glass of whiskey, Dane stood on the balcony of Lizzie's hotel room. Mere yards away, the waves of the Atlantic crashed on the shore beneath the moon.

The peaceful, romantic atmosphere was at odds with the turmoil pounding through his veins. How could he be so elated and filled with dread at the same time?

Lovers again, but destined to part. Again.

In fact, their lives were further apart now than they'd been before. Years ago, they'd been somewhat equals—ambitious and talented, ready to prove themselves to the world. Now she was famous all over the world, and he was…

Well, he was successful in his own right. He had championships and many, many wins to his credit. He was respected by his colleagues, friends and family.

But there was no escaping the fact that she was a star as bright as any in the sky, and he was a guy who tinkered with cars.

He sensed her behind him and turned to see her standing in the doorway, wearing one of the hotel's soft, white bathrobes. She held out her hand. "Come dance with me."

"You know I don't dance." But he went to her, of course. "I've never been coordinated."

Her lips turned up in a seductive smile as she tugged him inside, plucking the glass from his hand and setting it on a table. "Sure you are. All you have to do is shuffle your feet and hold me."

"Okay." He'd be crazy not to draw every single drop from every last moment he spent with her. Hearing the slow jazz filling the room, he realized the song was familiar and glanced over to see his MP3 player docked into the stereo system on the table near the TV.

Uh-oh.

The player had been in his jeans pocket and must have fallen out at some point during the frantic haste to get through clothes to skin earlier.

"You have a diverse music library," Lizzie said, sliding her arms around his neck.

"You think?" he returned, wincing.

"Lots of jazz, some hard rock and a pretty extensive playlist called LL, which has several song titles I recognize."

"I imagine you do."

"Want to comment on this compilation of my entire published musical history?"

"I told you I was a fan."

"And you bring my songs to the guys at the shop."

"Sure." His hands clenched around her waist, he concentrated on swaying back and forth without stumbling. "They're, you know, good songs."

"Are they?"

"Look, Lizzie's it's not—" He stopped when her soulful blue gaze hit his. Tears glittered in her eyes. "A big deal," he finished lamely.

"You really like my songs," she said.

"Yeah, yeah, I do." He stopped the pretense of dancing and pulled her tight against his chest. "Don't cry. You're killing me here."

"Why do you like them?" she mumbled, stubborn as always.

"Because they're yours. Because they help me feel better when things are crap." He closed his eyes and drew a deep breath as the familiar strum of an acoustic guitar ballad poured through the room. How many times had he listened to this song, alone in the dark and wishing she was there beside him?

Admitting aloud how much she meant to him was something he'd promised he'd never do again, but that vow turned to dust in the face of her touch, her tears and her poignant voice. "Because they make me feel close to you."

She kissed his chest, then the side of his neck, then his lips. "I'm here now." She cupped his face and kissed him again. "I'm here."

"WHEN DO YOU GO back on tour?" Dane asked Lizzie.

It was the night before the Daytona race, and they sat in the back corner booth of Porto Fino, a popular Italian restaurant that had hosted fans and legends of NASCAR for nearly twenty-five years.

"Not until the spring, but I start rehearsals March first, and I have several charity concerts to do in the meantime."

He'd known their time was limited, but hearing the news aloud was jarring. "Your schedule's as hectic as mine," he said, then sipped his wine to clear the tightness in his throat.

"I suppose so. You're off to California, then Vegas."

For once, he couldn't care less about the start of the season. "Yeah."

He drank in the sight of her in a dark blue sundress that matched her eyes, and recalled the week they'd spent together. Many days like the ones they'd had years before—her strumming her guitar and him working through calculations and setups for the car.

Nights in her suite. Nights of intimacy, intensity and indulgence.

He'd stayed away from the press functions she'd done for the race; she'd stayed away from the garage. They had a silent agreement that their jobs were too much reality.

But now reality was revving its engine too violently to ignore. His heart was heavy, and time seemed to speed up, the world spinning too fast, fighting against what he wanted most.

"I guess we should get back," she said, pushing her plate aside and looking as miserable as he felt. "You have a big day tomorrow."

He signaled the waiter for the check. "You, too."

After he paid the bill and they walked through the restaurant, he glided his hand down her waist, hugging her to his side. "Nashville and Mooresville aren't so far apart."

"No, but California and Tampa are. Which is where we'll each be next week."

"Don't worry. We'll figure something out."

Though what, he had no idea. His practical nature demanded he acknowledge a future for him and Lizzie wasn't possible, but his heart continued to hope. Could they really make up for the mistakes of the past?

They met up with Vince at the door, as he'd insisted on eating on the other side of the small restaurant to give them privacy. As a trio, they walked outside.

A portable TV camera's bright light greeted them, as well as a slick blonde reporter with a microphone. "Ms. Lancaster, are you looking forward to singing the national anthem tomorrow?"

Dane squinted into the light, but Lizzie, after an almost imperceptible gasp, smiled brightly. "Of course. It's the biggest event in racing. I was honored to be invited."

"A real treat for your fans." The reporter's gaze sharpened, flicked to Dane, then back to Lizzie. "I can't help but notice that James Allenton isn't by your side this weekend. Is there trouble in paradise?"

Dane clenched his jaw, but Lizzie just shook her head. "No. We're…fine." She squeezed Dane's arm. "Dane's an old friend and crew chief on PDQ's No. 432 car."

"Kelsey Kendall's car?" the reporter asked, swinging the microphone toward Dane. "The former open-wheel star?"

"Yes," Dane managed to say, though every muscle in his body had tightened to the breaking point. Lizzie and James were fine? When had she talked to him? "We're happy to have Kelsey among the NASCAR family. She'll be starting tenth in the race tomorrow."

The reporter smiled vapidly. "How sweet. Lizzie, is there any truth to the rumor that your recent hit 'Long Gone' is going to be featured in Joe Calponi's new film?"

"I've met with Mr. Calponi, so we'll see how things go in production."

"And what about you and James Allenton making the song a duet?"

For the first time, Lizzie looked annoyed. "'Long Gone' isn't a duet."

"That's enough," Vince said firmly from behind them. "Thank you. Ms. Lancaster needs to get to her next event."

With a decisive stride, Vince urged Dane and Lizzie forward, swerving around the reporter and cameraman, then they all climbed into the SUV parked just to the right of the restaurant's entrance.

Silently, they pulled out onto the highway.

As they rolled through the night, Dane tried to pretend the press ambush didn't matter, that their innuendos meant nothing, but the simmering anger in his blood wouldn't settle. "So you and James Allenton are doing just fine, huh?"

CHAPTER EIGHT

LIZZIE DIDN'T HAVE TO KNOW Dane as well as she did to spot the annoyance in his voice, and since she was pretty aggravated herself, her tone came out sharp. "What was I supposed to say?"

"That you were there with me."

"I can't announce that kind of thing impulsively to the press."

"Why not?"

"Because whether it's true or not, people think James and I are a couple. He's been involved with several people during the last few months, as well, and he's been discreet. He keeps his private life private—like I do."

Dane flung his arm toward the window. "*That* didn't seem private to me."

"It's simply a public face/private face thing. When your race car is junk, I imagine your driver doesn't announce that to the sports media." Her eyes narrowed. "What I want to know, is how the press knew we'd be in that restaurant, at that time? And the Calponi meeting, how did she know about that? I haven't told anybody except you and my staff."

Clearly still angry, Dane jerked out a shrug. "You met at the track. Anybody there could have told."

"But how did they know where we were having dinner? All the restaurants in this town, packed to the pier with fans, officials and crew, and a reporter just happens to find us?"

"Maybe they followed us."

From the front seat, Vince, very distinctly, cleared his throat.

"I think you've just insulted Vince's driving skills."

"Sorry, but it doesn't matter anyway." His eyes full of regret and determination, he met her gaze. "This isn't going to work, Lizzie."

"What isn't going to work?"

"This. *Us.*" His tone had taken on a distinct bite, and she knew his feelings—and maybe his ego—were hurt more than he wanted to admit by her not acknowledging him to the press. It seemed his practicality didn't necessarily extend to his love life. "I don't leave restaurants and encounter TV cameras and reporters."

The last bit made her drop her jaw. "You walk out of your hauler and encounter them every weekend."

"It's different."

"I'd like to know how."

"I'm doing my job then, and I'm essentially in my office when I talk to them."

"Well, how nice you have regular office hours," she said sarcastically, knowing that was anything but the truth. "Some of us don't have that luxury. When I'm in public, I'm fair game. It's not always fun, but that's the deal I signed up for."

"But I didn't."

She sucked in a surprised and painful breath and looked away. "You do if you want to be with me."

When he remained silent, her throat closed. "*If* you want to, that is," she said in the only whisper she could manage.

"We're too different. You belong with somebody like James Allenton."

She forced herself to look at him. "But I don't love James. I love you."

His hands clenched on the armrest, and something bright flashed in his eyes, then he shook his head. "You can't. And you won't once you get back to your real life. These last few days have been amazing, but we can't be together."

"Because you're scared to love me again."

"Because we're wrong for each other."

Her temper exploded. "That's complete crap! We're the *only* people for each other. Why do you think we're both still alone? We have friends and great jobs and all the stuff that's supposed to make us happy, and we're not."

"I'm—"

"Surely you're not going to tell me you're happy."

A muscle alongside his jaw pulsed. "I'm…fine."

"*Fine?*" she repeated incredulously. "You want to be fine? I want more. And, dammit, you're the one all that depends on. But if you want to be stubborn, then *fine.*"

She realized they were approaching the hotel entrance. At least she could escape the confines of the car, where she could feel him and breathe his scent and be close enough to touch him and, therefore, be tempted to beg.

She doubted she'd escape the crushing pressure in her chest so easily.

But he couldn't really be too afraid of taking a chance with her again? Big, strong, capable Dane Guthrie?

No way.

So she'd…

She closed her eyes to keep angry tears from falling. She'd have to find a way to reach him, and, in the meantime, she had an important performance. No way was she letting down those race fans who'd supported her career over all these years.

Before the SUV had come to a complete stop, or Dane or Vince could move, she flung open the door. "Good luck tomorrow," she said to Dane, casting one last, furious glare at him. "I know at least *that's* important to you." Then she slammed the door and stormed into the hotel.

USED TO Lizzie's hot temper, Vince descended calmly from the car so the valet could take over. Knowing her pain as well as his own, he glared at Dane Guthrie as he climbed out of the backseat. "If you don't find a way to fix this, you're a damn fool."

WHAT ELSE COULD HE DO but go back to work?

He avoided Lizzie on race morning, which was easy to do with all the fans, media and security guards surrounding her. He bowed his head while she sang and tried desperately to remember the camber and tire pressure on the race car, then his multiplication tables from fourth grade—anything to block out the sound of her voice.

Nothing worked. He walked to the pit box with a

stone in his stomach that never eased, so he was barely able to do his job. His precious, all-important job that he was using as an excuse to keep his distance from the love of his life.

On the positive side, Kelsey and Bart finished in the top fifteen.

"We'll get 'em next week in California," Bart said as they walked back to the garage area from pit road.

"Yeah," Dane returned with little enthusiasm.

Bart clapped him on the shoulder. "Always the perfectionist. Where's Lizzie? Bet she could cheer you up."

"Yeah," Dane said, feeling worse than ever. "If I hadn't pissed her off."

"Oh, man. What'd ya do that for?"

Fear, he thought, but didn't say so aloud. He simply shook his head.

"So, come up with an apology," Bart said. "Get her to forgive you."

His temper and emotional defenses battling, Dane stopped and stared at the driver. "Will you ever forgive your father?"

Bart's teasing expression vanished. "Why should I? He's never done one damn thing—" He stopped and hung his head, clearly trying to get a hold of his own temper. "My sister said his shrink has him writing a journal, but he'll never be able to explain or excuse what he's done to us." He sighed. "You don't want my advice on love and commitment anyway."

"I shouldn't have brought up your family. It's none of my business."

Bart met his gaze. "You need to fight for Lizzie. You never know how long you'll have with her."

As Bart turned on his heel and headed in the opposite direction, Dane couldn't block out the truth of the other man's advice or forget Lizzie's words.

All the next week, he dwelled on her confession and his own feelings.

She loved him, and he was afraid. Somewhere along the way, he'd even stopped denying he loved her, and that made him even more afraid.

He'd promised himself that he couldn't fall under her spell ever again. He couldn't place his happiness in the hands of someone else. He had to make his own way. Create his own success.

Professionally, he had. He was doing what he'd dreamed of. He'd risen to the top of his profession as few could expect.

Otherwise, he was…fine.

But Lizzie was right. Fine was no way to live. It was acceptable. Satisfactory. Adequate. And beneath him.

Certainly not worthy of the man who'd loved the amazing Lizzie Lancaster all his life. He needed her. He had to have her to be happy, and he was tired of trying to fool himself into believing that everything inside him didn't belong to her.

"Is something wrong with the car, chief?"

It was Saturday morning, and he was driving his team from the hotel to the track in California. One of his mechanics in the backseat had posed the dreaded question.

"It's fine," Dane said.

"You seem…edgy."

Remembering he'd asked the same thing at Daytona, Dane very nearly smiled. "I'm miserable."

The mechanic exchanged a look with his colleague sitting beside him, who shrugged and shook his head. "Oh. Sorry."

"It's okay. I'm gonna do something about it."

So after Kelsey's last practice session, Dane handed his car chief his laptop and notebook and told him he was going to Vegas for the night.

Briefly glimpsing the shock and disbelief in his team's eyes, Dane strode from the track and drove directly to the airport, where he caught the next flight. He knew Lizzie was performing a charity concert at one of the luxury hotels on the strip.

He didn't hope to make the show on time, or even anticipate getting a ticket, since his Internet search told him the event had been sold out for months, but he had one card up his sleeve that would certainly have the pit bosses at the casino nodding with admiration.

He had Vince Malleta's cell-phone number.

Lizzie had given it to him the week before in case he needed to get in touch with her. Vince was always by her side.

Dane sincerely hoped the driver didn't bear a grudge.

Or have the urge to fit him with concrete blocks before he'd heard Dane's side of the story. Thankfully, either because there was a mushy heart beneath all those muscles or he sensed Dane's sincerity, Vince let him in by way of the loading dock's back door.

Lizzie was already on stage.

Dane's palms grew damp as Vince led him past thick ropes of wires, stage hands dealing with props and technicians managing sound and lights. He hadn't watched her perform live in well over a decade. From the wings, with her graced by the spotlight, her hair a flame-colored halo, he was filled with regret that he hadn't been there for each and every one.

When she sang "Long Gone," he imagined he was the only one who heard the catch in her voice.

He had to make sure she changed that depressing ending ASAP.

While the notes of the song trailed away, Vince urged him toward Lizzie's dressing room, where he could wait with his nerves and the offering of roses he'd brought.

Along with his heart.

The door cracked, and he heard her voice. "Thanks so much, guys. Great show. Vince, can we be ready to go in twenty minutes?"

She whipped around the door a moment later, leaning back against it and closing her eyes.

"It's no wonder you're still my favorite singer," he said quietly.

Her eyes flew open, then she blinked, as if she couldn't believe what she saw. "Dane?"

He extended the bundle of roses. "I was an idiot."

"What?" She stopped, took the roses and inhaled their scent. "This is…what're you doing here? Aren't you supposed to be in California?"

"Yeah, but I'd rather be with you." He took the roses and set them on the nearby table, then pulled her into his arms before she could remember she was furious at him. "I love you."

Her deep blue gaze, hurt but hopeful, flew to his. "Since when?"

He hugged her tight and prayed she wouldn't push him away. "Since about the tenth grade."

She leaned into him, clutching him around his waist. "It's about time you realized it. I've been completely miserable all week, trying to figure out how to make you see we're meant to be together and get past that stubborn practicality of yours. But so far I haven't— Hang on…" As she trailed off, her formidable temper sprang, and she jerked back. "A few days ago you said we were wrong for each other. We couldn't be together."

He winced. "I think I already said I was an idiot, but I can say it again."

She jabbed her finger in the center of his chest. "You bet you can, chief. I've been miserable and worried and—"

He silenced her with a long, deep kiss. It was the only thing he could think of to do to soothe her anger, but the benefits for him were pretty spectacular, too. "We can make it work," he said as he was forced to part from her for air. "Relationships are about commitment and balance."

Apparently realizing they were on the same page, she wrapped her arms around his neck. "I guess they are."

"All those years ago, I *was* scared. I didn't see any way our worlds could mesh. And when they didn't, I held myself apart, so nobody could hurt me again." He kissed her forehead to soften his words. "Especially you."

"And I used your ultimatum to follow my own dreams and justify leaving you behind."

He smiled, and for the first time in a long time, the feeling was genuine. "But I've learned—" He stopped as she lifted her eyebrows. "Okay, *we've* learned a thing or two over the last fourteen years, and that includes the confidence that we can do anything we set our minds to." He stroked his hand down her silky, fiery hair. "I'm not afraid anymore. And I'll make whatever sacrifices I have to so we can be together the rest of our lives."

Her eyes bright with love, the way he'd always dreamed of them, she cocked her head. "Well, after that thoughtful, impassioned speech, I think I should at least be able to come up with some lyrics, a decent chorus, maybe even including a melody that expresses how much this moment means to me."

His heart leapt. "Another song? Maybe one with a happy ending this time?"

"Oh, you bet." She nodded and smiled. "We'll call it…'I'm Fine'."

"I'm—" He scowled. "Very funny. You're going to hold that against me for the next fifty years, aren't you?"

She tucked her head between his neck and shoulder and sighed. "Absolutely."

"Whatever, but you *are* going to break up with James Allenton, right?"

EPILOGUE

WHEN HOLLYWOOD PRODUCER Joe Calponi's film was nominated for multiple Oscars the next year, Lizzie was inspired to write a new verse to the song, which she performed in concert and on the big awards night among the Hollywood stars.

In not-so-great news, Lizzie learned her manager Ronnie had leaked the information about the meeting with the movie producer and where she and Dane were having dinner in Daytona Beach. The betrayal was too much for her to accept, so she parted ways with him.

As well as James Allenton. He began dating a blonde runway model who was almost as hot as him.

Lizzie and Dane announced their engagement a few weeks after the breakup.

Maybe Dane and Lizzie's path to understanding each other, to believing in love and happily ever after had been a winding one, but they'd found it nonetheless. And whatever detours they had taken, Lizzie knew they'd always find their way to reach each other.

'Cause that was just how love did its magical, miraculous thing.

* * * * *

Chasing the Dream

Abby Gaines

For my brother Charles—love always.

CHAPTER ONE

NOTHING LIKE SLAMMING into a wall at a hundred and eighty miles an hour to sharpen a guy's focus.

From the first, jarring impact, Jeb Stallworth did what he had to, running on instinct. Steered the No. 464 car away from the idiot who'd knocked him into the wall. Braced himself for a pasting from the No. 502 car coming up fast in his rearview mirror. Tried to figure a way to get this machine back into its line so he could grab a win here at Daytona. A win that, ten seconds ago, had appeared his for the taking.

He'd never won at Daytona before, and now— damn! there it was. Into the wall again. Jeb lurched in the confined cockpit of his car. Typical Eli Ward, always too light on the No. 502's brakes. Although Jeb's brain knew that the SAFER barriers compulsory at NASCAR-sanctioned tracks were far easier on his body than the old-style concrete walls, they weren't any more pleasant to hit.

Dammit, he was airborne. Not much a driver could do once his wheels left the ground, not even a NASCAR champion. Weird how turning upside down seemed to happen so slowly…. The car came down on its front bumper…

Huh, been a while since I did a double roll.

How many times had he crashed in the twenty-some years since he'd started racing a midget as a fifteen-year-old with special dispensation? Since then he'd raced bikes, dragsters, dune buggies. Pretty much anything on wheels. Remember the time he crashed that dune buggy in the Sahara?

Right on cue, the crash played in his head, like a movie. Distracting him from the fact his car was now going airborne for a third time, and his crew chief was yelling in his headphones, with something less than his usual professional aplomb.

Guess this crash looks really bad.

Jeb caught a glimpse of fans on their feet, some with hands clamped over eyes or mouth, others with their mouths wide-open, as if they were shrieking.

Heck, how bad *was* this crash?

Images of other smashes pelted through his mind at full speed. There was that huge one in Dallas that had sucked in both Jeb and his best friend, Pat Rivers. Pat was gone now, killed in a boating accident, ironically enough. Damn, Jeb still missed him. At least Pat had died knowing he'd lived life to the fullest. Not just on the race track, but with his family.

Jeb searched the footage playing through his head for some indication that he, too, had extracted the maximum from life.

He saw more crashes. But plenty of podium finishes, plenty of trophies. He was a champion, and there weren't many guys who could say that. Ah, there was his personal life now. Look at those gorgeous women he'd dated. There was, uh, Mandy…or was it Millie?

Mary? What the heck? For the life of him, he couldn't remember one single name.

He knew his helmet hadn't been dislodged, so why was his memory blanking? Jeb didn't want to remove his gloved hands from the wheel to check. He couldn't steer through midair, but something about gripping the wheel made him feel he had a say in how this thing ended.

Why couldn't he remember the women he'd dated? Why didn't he feel even a flicker of loss?

If a guy's life was going to flash before his eyes, shouldn't it be a little more meaningful?

EARLY MONDAY MORNING, Jeb lay on the couch in front of the fire in the beamed living room of his home on Lake Norman. It was still dark enough outside that the view of the lake didn't draw his eye.

He hadn't slept much, and though he had only a sprained right wrist to show for that spectacular crash, which had culminated in a prosaic, right-side-up landing, he didn't feel like doing anything more than watching the replay of yesterday's race.

On his wide-screen TV with surround sound this time, not in his head.

He hadn't even needed to go to the hospital at Daytona, and the doctor at the track's infield care center had said with a shrug that Jeb would doubtless be driving in next Sunday's NASCAR Sprint Cup Series race.

Great news.

So why was he lying here, staring into the flames with all the energy of a poached egg?

He knew why.

Not because he was ticked off over being robbed of that elusive victory at Daytona. But because when he'd landed back on all four wheels and stuck an arm out the window to tell the safety crew—and the millions of fans—he was okay, he'd wondered if *okay* was enough.

If he was missing out on something important.

"Jeb? You awake? It's me." A female voice broke through the rising excitement of the commentators on the TV.

Jeb muted the sound. "In here." Already the sense of futility was lifting; he stood, just as Cara Rivers appeared in the doorway, wearing the pale green scrubs that served as her uniform in her job as a labor and delivery nurse. She carried two cups of takeout coffee, mocha for her, latte for him.

"I thought you might still be sleeping off the injuries you sustained setting a new record for in-car acrobatics," she teased as she crossed the plush gray carpet.

"Anything to give the fans a thrill." Something stirred inside Jeb at her smile, as it always had done, since the day he met her. After she'd married Pat, his best friend, he'd reined in his reactions, of course, keeping their relationship purely platonic. But these days…

Her kiss landed somewhere near his chin. He considered dragging her into his arms and kissing her the way he had once before, long ago.

Whoa. The emotional aftermath of the accident was going to his head. And other places. He planted himself back on the leather couch. "Kids okay?" he asked.

"The sitter was getting them out of bed when I left. You'd think it'd be easy, since we follow the same routine every morning, but there were the usual grumbles all around." Cara put the coffees on the table and settled next to him. Even in her scrubs and sneakers, with her blond hair tied back in a short ponytail, she was sexier than any woman he knew.

"How's the wrist?" Her fingers trailed lightly over the bandage.

Jeb's veins thrummed beneath her touch. Platonic was definitely off the menu today.

"A sprain, no big deal." He turned his hand over and caught her fingers in his, ignoring the pain the movement caused. Her fingers were slender, but strong. "Had Ryder worried, though."

Ryder McGraw, his crew chief, had said it was the biggest smash he'd seen in years.

Cara chortled, and she sounded like a teenager, not the thirty-four-year-old woman she was. She'd been eighteen when they met, to his nineteen. In terms of maturity, though, of knowing what she wanted, she'd been way ahead of him. "Like you don't have a rubber skull," she joked.

"It was a bad smash," he said. "The car was totaled."

"When you wreck a car, you do it good." She grabbed the remote, turned up the sound. "Let's watch it again."

Jeb stifled a pang of irritation. Sure, Cara was voicing his own laidback thoughts. But he couldn't help remembering how every time Pat had the tiniest fender bender on the track, she'd be sobbing and covering her eyes. So worried she wouldn't sleep for two nights afterward. Clinging to Pat as if he was the most precious thing in the world.

"I could have been seriously injured," he said, not liking the whine in his own voice.

"Yeah, yeah." She waved a hand. "I can't believe Garrett Clark wasn't penalized for putting you in the wall."

At least she cared enough to worry about his position in the points standing.

"Just because he's gorgeous and the reigning champion, he gets away with murder," she continued.

She thought Garrett Clark was gorgeous? Jeb stiffened. "I'll show Clark who's boss next Sunday," he promised.

"A grudge match, how mature." She peeled the lid off her mocha and inspected it. Then she closed her eyes and inhaled the chocolaty caffeine aroma. "Ah, the first cup of the day. First cup of *real* coffee," she amended. "I choked down some instant before I left."

He envisaged her in her kitchen, grimacing over a substandard brew. In his mind, her hair was sleep-tousled and she wore very short pajamas, and nothing else, which he knew was unlikely in the depths of a Charlotte winter. Still, it made for an intriguing picture.

After he'd got past the shock of losing Pat in that boating accident, Jeb had realized he still wanted Cara…and now she was free. But he'd been in no hurry to do anything about it. They'd both needed time to mourn Pat. And Jeb's racing kept him so busy, it was less complicated to avail himself of more casual female companionship.

But he'd always figured that he and Cara might end up together one day. Spooky that he'd just been wondering what was missing, and Cara should turn up in his living room.

Maybe what he was missing was the right woman to share his life.

Maybe the right woman was right in front of him.

Maybe *one day* was now. Today.

CHAPTER TWO

THE THOUGHT ROCKED JEB, first with its life-altering implications, then with its simplicity.

Why not go after the meaning that his life lacked,
starting now? He and Cara would be great together and
he was crazy about the kids. They could move in tomorrow!

Mentally, he applied the brakes. Cara was naturally
cautious. She'd become his best friend in her own right,
so making a move on her would be a major rocking of
the boat. A risk. *If you don't take a risk, you don't win.*

Still, no point jumping the green flag. First up, Jeb
needed to know where she was at in her love life.

He picked up his coffee and took a considered sip
through the hole in the lid. "How was your date on Saturday night?" He'd encouraged Cara to get back into
the swing of dating recently—it would be painfully
ironic if she'd fallen hard for some other guy.

She blinked at the change of subject. "Pretty good
for a first date. Mike's a nice guy."

"Did he—" *Kiss you? Make love to you?* No way
could he ask that. "Take you someplace nice?"

"An Italian restaurant uptown. Rather fancy."

"So…do you like him?" Jeb wasn't used to dancing

around a subject. His instinct when he saw a gap was to drive straight through.

"I do." Cara smoothed her scrubs over her thighs. "He asked me to dinner on Wednesday, so I guess he likes me, too." A little smile played on her lips.

Was she serious about this Mike character? Dammit, Jeb's career, his life, depended on his making the right move at the right time out on the track. He should have known better than to leave his personal life to chance.

He put down his coffee. Twisting on the couch, he grabbed Cara's left hand with his. Rubbed her finger where Pat's wedding ring used to be. She'd taken it off when she started dating those accountants and teachers he'd been arrogant enough not to feel threatened by. "Cara, you've always been special to me, you know that, right?"

"Of course," she said lightly, setting her cup beside his. "And vice versa. I don't know what the kids and I would have done without you after Pat died."

"Even before that," he said. "Long before. I met you first, remember."

Way to sound like a spoiled brat. But it was true. He'd met Cara at the Nashville track when he was a rookie in the NASCAR Camping World Truck Series. Which meant he'd known her longer than she'd known Pat.

"Nashville," she said, proving they were on the same wavelength. She fiddled with the edge of a cushion. "You were so cocky, I didn't know what to make of you."

She'd found him attractive, regardless. Jeb hadn't hesitated to ask her on a date. He'd taken her to a French restaurant in downtown Nashville, about ten rungs higher than where he usually took a first date. Because from the get-go it had been clear Cara was different. That she knew what she wanted and wouldn't accept less.

Beneath his up-and-coming-NASCAR-star cool, he'd been daunted.

"We had dinner at Le Bon Gourmet." He couldn't believe he still recalled the name of the place. "Then afterward, we took a stroll down Honky Tonk Row, remember?"

That was all he intended to say, because Cara valued good manners. A gentleman wouldn't remind her how they'd slipped into a darkened doorway and, to the accompaniment of country music wafting from the bar next door, shared that incredible kiss.

At least, a gentleman wouldn't remind her *outright*.

"Um, sure." Her cheeks were pink. Oh, yeah, she remembered.

This was all going exactly the way it should.

Jeb allowed himself a moment's distraction, recollecting that kiss as clearly as if it was yesterday. His gaze landed on Cara's lips, the same sweet curve that had driven him wild—

"You must have kissed a million women since then," she said.

He frowned. "Not a million."

"But you've lost count, right?" she said blithely.

"Uh…" Okay, this wasn't his finest moment. He had indeed lost count of the number of women he'd kissed. But it was never too late for a guy to cut back.

"Whereas I can number the men I've kissed since then on one hand," she continued.

Did that mean she'd been kissing other guys, those guys she was dating? *Of course she has.* She was a grown woman with…needs. His mind shied away from her meeting those needs with some accountant. His hands clenched on his knees.

Shouldn't Cara be a little jealous that he'd kissed so many women?

"Pathetic, huh?" She grinned.

Jeb spread his fingers, forced them to relax. "I think it's admirable."

"Is that a double standard I see?"

"No way. You and Pat were together twelve years, and it's taken time for you to be ready to—" *get back on the horse* "—resume a single life. Now that you are, you'll have dozens of guys lining up." He might need to put some work into getting to the front of the line, but didn't he do that for a living? With considerable success?

She laughed as she picked up her mocha. "You're such a charmer. Why hasn't one of your myriad admirers snapped you up?"

Jeb shifted, and caught a hint of the jasmine perfume she'd worn as long as he'd known her. If he leaned across just a few inches, he could kiss her…. He cleared his throat. "I'm glad you asked."

Cara eyed him curiously over the rim of her cup.

Faint morning sun had begun to lighten the room, giving Jeb the sense of a new beginning.

"That crash yesterday," he said, "started me thinking about how life can be short."

She froze, then wrapped both hands around her cup. "You weren't in any real danger."

She spoke so emphatically, he lost track of what he was saying. "Sure, I was fine." He found his groove again. "But accidents can happen anywhere, and if you're not on a race track, you don't have the benefit of a helmet and a roll cage and millions of dollars of safety features."

Cara's face shuttered. He shouldn't have alluded to Pat.

"What's your point?" she asked tightly.

"My point—" Jeb groped for words through a fog of uncertainty "—is that it's important to make the most of life. Like Pat always did."

Cara nodded. That was better. Jeb warmed to his theme. "I love NASCAR, it's been everything I could hope for. But there are other things that should mean something to a man, and it's time I paid them some attention."

Her forehead creased. "Such as?"

She of all people should know what he was talking about. Jeb felt a speed-wobble of doubt. The best way to get past a speed-wobble was to floor it. "Love," he said. "Family. I've realized those things are missing from my life."

Cara's lips pursed. He said quickly, "Yeah, I'm a slow learner. I've had enough dates over the years to take my mind off the serious stuff. But the fact is, I want it."

"You want what?" She clutched the coffee cup to her chest. "You're not making a lot of sense, Jeb."

His next words were so radical in the context of his life, he had trouble persuading his mouth to utter them. At last, he got them out. "I want to get married. I want to have a family."

Cara stared.

Then she laughed.

CHAPTER THREE

JEB HAD TO BE JOKING—Cara was aware her laughter had an edge of hysteria. She pushed off the couch, slopping coffee over the edge of her cup. She was so disturbed, she didn't stop to wipe it up, just concentrated on putting a good ten feet of space between her and Jeb.

"Did they check you for a concussion yesterday?" she asked.

"Of course," Jeb said impatiently. "I wasn't unconscious, not even for a second. Would you mind telling me what's so funny?"

His rigid posture told her she'd offended him. Jeb was turning *sensitive?* Foreboding swept her. She didn't like this, not one bit.

She strove for lightheartedness. "There are one or two things I like to think of as constants in my life. Like the sun rising in the morning, watching NASCAR on TV on Sundays and…and you being Charlotte's most eligible bachelor." She found herself blinking hard. "You can't go dropping a bombshell like that."

He eased back, one arm extended along the back of the couch, his fingers drumming the cushion. "I only just figured it out myself."

For some reason, the way he took up so much space on the couch riled her. "Getting married isn't a spur-of-the-moment decision," she said sharply. "You can't decide you want a family one minute, and hey, presto, your life has *meaning* the next."

"Why not, if I've found the right person?"

Her stomach dipped; she should have eaten breakfast before she left home. "Have you?"

For a long moment, he didn't answer. "Maybe."

Cara had no idea who he'd dated lately. Jeb never seemed to take much interest in his own love life, so nor did she. "Are you…in love?"

His fingers stopped their drumming. "Define *in love.*"

She thought about her years with Pat, and the years he'd been gone. "I guess it's when the other person matters more to you than you do. When you'll give up everything for them. When losing them—" her voice caught "—is the worst thing you can imagine." She'd had that love for Pat; she would always have it for her children.

He frowned as he leaned forward, hands clasped between his knees. "That's just your definition, right? It's not in the dictionary?"

Her laugh was shaky. "My definition. But I stand by it." As his frown deepened, she relaxed enough to perch on the arm of a leather recliner. "So…if you haven't figured out the in-love part, your playboy lifestyle might be safe a while yet."

"I'm not exactly a playboy these days."

Her gazed flicked to a framed photograph on the wall: Jeb being awarded the NASCAR Camping World

Truck Series trophy a couple of years ago. A well-known supermodel clung to his arm.

"I spend more time with you and your kids than I do on hot dates," he protested. "You could say," he continued deliberately, "you guys are already my family."

Pictures flashed through her mind—Jeb helping Dylan fix his bike, taking Shane to soccer, admiring Lucy's Lego creation. Sitting with Cara over a coffee at the end of the day.

They had a friendship that was rare between a man and a woman who weren't…involved. When Pat died, it had been natural for them to draw even closer together.

She couldn't bear to lose that friendship, part of the bedrock of her life without Pat. But no way would things stay the same if Jeb got married.

Unless—the thought hit her—unless he was trying to suggest that *she*…

The recliner rocked beneath her, the whole world seemed unsteady on its axis this morning. Cara pressed her sneakers into the carpet, anchoring herself.

She'd recognized sixteen years ago that she and Jeb weren't an option. And he still radiated that undercurrent of danger she'd sensed the first time they met. She'd been attracted to it back then, of course. But one kiss—one *incredible* kiss—had told her she couldn't handle a guy like him.

Thankfully, he'd been scared off, too, unready for the intensity that kiss had promised. Then he'd introduced her to Pat, who was everything she wanted. Who'd loved her with the gentle certainty she needed.

Pat had been the logical choice, but much more than that. She'd loved him back, with all her heart....

She'd put her brief attraction to Jeb behind her years ago. So if he had some wacky idea about dragging her and her kids into his latest whim, he could forget it.

"You've been a wonderful buddy to my kids and we do see you as part of the family," she admitted. She chose her next words carefully, in case she was completely wrong about this. "But, Jeb, you need to face facts. You're not father material."

A millisecond of incredulous silence. Then Jeb shot to his feet. "*What* did you say?" He advanced on her.

Cara leaped up from the recliner. "Quit *looming,*" she ordered.

Of course, he kept right on looming, taking full advantage of the six inches he had on her. "I want to know what you mean."

Cara rubbed her palms against her thighs. "Being a parent isn't about swooping in for the fun moments, then leaving again. You never have to deal with the hard stuff or the boring stuff." The things Pat had delighted in. "The kids adore you, and no wonder. You feed them junk, you let them run riot over the furniture, you think bedtime is a moving target—"

"They need to let off steam sometimes, to take a break from all those rules and routines you're so fond of," he retorted.

Oof! Cara felt as if he'd punched her in the stomach. Was he calling her a bad mother? She wrapped her arms around her middle and said with an effort, "Those rules and routines give them structure and security. Two things they sorely need with their dad gone. Two things you know nothing about. Any woman with sense—" if he thought Cara was such a prison warden of a mother, he obviously didn't have her in mind "—will see that and run a mile."

"You're every bit as narrow-minded as you were at eighteen," he accused her. "There was always only one way to live life, and that was your way."

"It was Pat's way, too," she pointed out.

"Yeah, but he never thought everyone else should be like him," Jeb said.

He strode past her to the oversized fireplace. She loved that fireplace, with its slate surround. A couple of times the kids had "camped out" in front of it—the Persian rug still bore traces of the s'mores they'd roasted in the middle of the night.

He added a log to the fire; it thudded against the grate. "You and I have one thing in common," he said.

"Is that so?"

Jeb stared into the flames, licking hungrily at the log. "I'm as good as you are at getting what I want."

Something at Cara's core read his words as a threat. Her whole body tightened, a primitive defense mechanism. Her mind shrieked, *retreat*. "I came here to cheer you up about missing out at Daytona," she said. "Not to criticize you or have you knock the way I'm raising my kids. Let's just drop the subject."

"Trying to make the rules for me now, too?" he demanded. "That might work with the kids, it might even have worked with Pat—"

She gasped.

"But I've always made my own choices and stuck with them."

Cara felt a strange pain in her chest, as if something was chipping away at her heart. "Jeb, please, let's stop. I don't want to argue with you. You're my best friend, and I don't want that to change. I don't want anything to change."

He stared at her a long moment. Then he sighed, a slow release of breath. "Sometimes I think you're the bravest woman I know. Other times, you're one hundred percent pure chicken."

"I *was* going to say thanks, till you got to that last part." She attempted a joke, and the atmosphere lightened.

"Ignore me," he said. "I have a sore wrist, I just blew my first win at Daytona and I've spent too much time thinking."

That sounded more like the Jeb she knew.

"Hey, I can ignore you," she said lightly. Aware that she couldn't. That she never had been able to.

JEB ESCORTED CARA out to her SUV, holding the door open until she'd clipped her seat belt and buzzed down the window.

"Talk to you tomorrow?" The hint of a question in her voice. Normally it was a given that he would call her, or she would call him, but there was still a strain in the air.

"Of course." He saluted. "Give the kids a big hug for me."

Her shoulders eased, and she started the engine. "Will do. See ya."

As he watched her car disappear down his driveway, he felt as if he'd done another triple flip, this time without benefit of a roll cage. As if he'd been pummeled into pavement.

So much for the fanciful notion he'd had of Cara and the kids moving in tomorrow. She didn't think he had it in him to be a good father! He'd been deluding himself with some idiotic fantasy of a family that would never be his.

On his way into the house, Jeb stubbed his toe on the doorstep; he cursed. Cara still saw him the way she had when she was a teenager. But she wasn't the only one living in the past. This…this *crush* he had on her was based on…what? The memory of a kiss?

Pathetic.

Back in the living room, the fire had died away. Jeb prodded it with the poker, and wisps of smoke rose up the chimney. He wanted a wife and family. It was time, and he wasn't about to change his mind.

But Cara wasn't the woman for him.

He would find someone else.

A woman who would take him as he was, with faith that he could become a great husband and father…even if he had some work to do. He wasn't afraid of work.

He turned off the TV, still playing yesterday's race, and walked over to the window. A duck waddled across the bottom of the lawn, then splashed into the lake.

Jeb's throat felt scratchy; he rubbed it. Sixteen years of thinking Cara Jenkinson Rivers was the ultimate woman wouldn't be erased easily. But he'd made paradigm shifts before. A race driver always had to adapt.

He and Cara would still be friends, of course, and he'd do anything for the kids. But this immature, unrequited passion, which he clearly hadn't given much rational thought since he was nineteen years old…

"It's over," he announced to the sun, to the pale morning sky. To the frolicking duck. "This thing stops now."

CHAPTER FOUR

CARA WISHED SHE'D NEVER said a word about Jeb's sudden enthusiasm for settling down. He probably would have forgotten about it in five minutes, but, no, she'd jumped in with her kneejerk reaction. And now, even though they'd backed away from the argument, tension gnawed at her as they talked on the phone on Tuesday night. She found herself wrapping the phone cord tighter and tighter around her index finger.

Jeb wasn't his usual self, either. They talked perfunctorily about the kids, about her day at the hospital, about the press interview he'd done that morning. Nothing more personal.

"I'd better go," Cara said after ten unsatisfactory minutes. "I need to call around and find a sitter for tomorrow night. Michelle—" her regular sitter "—has a wedding shower."

"You going anywhere interesting?" Jeb asked in the polite, distant tone that was getting on her nerves.

"Another date with Mike," she admitted.

A pause. "I'll babysit for you," he offered.

"Really?" Gladness rushed through her. "That would be wonderful." If he was still willing to look after the kids, maybe she hadn't entirely messed up their friendship. She disentangled her finger from the cord. "Is seven o'clock okay?"

"No problem," he said. "It's a date."

The awkwardness came back.

"You know what I mean," Jeb said.

JEB PULLED INTO the driveway of Cara's home near Mooresville at seven o'clock on Wednesday, right on time. He crunched along the limestone pebble path toward the two-story farmhouse she and Pat had bought soon after they married. They'd done it up and added to it over the years, but the place had never lost its cozy, family feel.

Lucy, at five years old the youngest of the Rivers clan, was kneeling on the window seat in the living room, waving at Jeb. He waved back, then blew her an extravagant kiss, and she collapsed into giggles.

Cara would probably complain he was getting her overexcited.

"Uncle Jeb!" Shane, seven years old, threw himself at Jeb as he walked in the door. "You gotta see what I made in art today."

"You're right, I *have* to," Jeb said with deliberate grammatical correctness as he ruffled Shane's hair. See, he could set a good example for the kids. Not father material, huh?

"Come see Mama." Lucy appeared in the living room doorway. "She looks pretty."

"She always does," Jeb said easily, following her. "Hey, Dylan."

Dylan, Cara's oldest son, barely looked up from his electronic game. "I just need to finish this level—if I kill three more aliens, I get a diamond sword."

"No problem." Jeb had played enough of those games to appreciate how painful it was to quit when you were ahead.

"Hi, Jeb." Cara spoke from the doorway.

Jeb turned. And tried not to stare. She had her hair in some kind of sophisticated "do," pulled back from her face and pinned sleekly against her head. She wore a fitted dress, electric blue silk.

"Is that new?" Did asking about her dress count as just friends? Or was it more personal than he was allowed to be under his new policy of keeping his distance?

Cara would know, with her penchant for rules.

She wrinkled her nose. "It's been a long time since I bought any new clothes, but I saw this and…what do you think?"

"Very nice," he said in understatement. He decided against kissing her on the cheek the way he normally would. Lately, those kisses had been landing at the corner of her mouth.

She'd leaned forward to meet him; now, she faltered. "Uh, thanks for stepping in at short notice."

"You know I can't miss a chance to be with the kids." He tilted his head to one side. "That dress isn't sitting right." Not that he was looking.

"It's not done up." She tugged at the skirt. "The zipper stuck. Would you mind?"

She turned her back on him, exposing a deep vee of pale skin, and a lacy black bra strap. It wasn't the first time Jeb had zipped Cara up. Which meant he knew she normally wore white or pale pink underwear. What was with the black?

He reached for the zipper…then realized he couldn't touch it, couldn't touch *her,* without entertaining a visual image that would undermine his decision to move on.

"Is there a problem?" She peered over her shoulder.

"Hey, Dylan." He managed to get the boy's attention. "I have a challenge for you."

The nine-year-old thrived on competition, the way his father had, the way Jeb did. He sprang off the couch, his diamond sword forgotten. "What is it?"

"You know my team had the fastest pit of the day at Daytona, right?"

"Twelve point six seconds," Dylan said. When it came to NASCAR, no detail escaped him.

"I bet you can't fix your mom's zipper in less time," Jeb said.

Cara's shoulders tensed.

"Easy," Dylan said, disgusted. As he grabbed the zipper, Jeb barely had time to hope the kid's hands were clean before the metal rasped into place. Removing that disturbing glimpse of black lace.

"Impressive performance," Jeb said. "There may be a place for you on my over-the-wall team someday." Dylan high-fived him, then returned to his game.

"The kids have already eaten," Cara said, an edge to her voice. "There's some fish pie in the oven if you'd like it."

"Great."

She was a wonderful cook. As they headed to the kitchen, he tried to ignore her legs in that dress, and focused instead on the incredible smell coming from the oven. *That* was the hunger he should be feeding.

His desire for Cara, on the other hand, needed to be starved. Which was why he wasn't about to kiss her cheek, zip up her dress, or let her hand brush his as they both reached into the crockery shelf for a plate—he whipped his hand away just as she did the same. The plate fell to the floor and broke cleanly in two.

"Sorry," he said, "I thought you had it."

"I thought you did."

He crouched down to pick up the pieces. Cara passed him some newspaper; he wrapped the broken china and dropped it in the trash. Then he took the dustpan from her to sweep up any invisible china dust. The whole process felt so homey, so normal, with the added fillip of the quickening of his pulse that invariably happened around her.

Not anymore.

"So, you're seeing Mike again already," he said, overloud. "Sounds serious."

She pulled the fish pie from the oven and set it on the counter. "Hmm."

What was that supposed to mean?

"You've only had one date," he reminded her. "Might be too soon to get serious."

"Hmm." She rinsed a serving spoon under the faucet.

"Are you *sleeping* with him?" Damn, he wasn't going to ask that.

Cara let out a little squawk as she glanced over her shoulder toward the living room. "Of course not," she hissed, outraged but half laughing. For all her conservativeness, Jeb could always make her laugh with his audacity. He loved—liked—that he could bring out that side of her.

His heart slowed from the sudden, rapid acceleration brought on by the thought of her sleeping with Mike. "Of course not," he agreed, relieved. "You're not casual about anything, especially sex."

"Jeb!" She pressed her palms to her cheeks.

He laughed. "I can't believe it, you're a mother of three, yet you blush scarlet at the word *sex*." He said it with relish.

"Because this is not an appropriate conversation to be having with the kids close by," she scolded.

Doubtless another black mark against his parenting potential. Jeb sobered. "So is Mike *father material?*"

"The kids like him—he's Shane's soccer coach." She served a helping of fish pie onto an unbroken plate.

"*That* Mike?" Jeb had seen the guy at the games. He wouldn't have pegged him as Cara's type. *That was when I thought I was her type.* "The skinny guy?"

She cocked her head. "I wouldn't say he's skinny. He told me he works out."

Jeb had an irrational desire to challenge Mike to a bench-press contest.

"I think he's nice-looking," Cara continued.

The guy had dark hair, like Jeb. He was taller than Jeb.

"I guess some women like that lanky look," he said.

She laughed, and he wanted to cover that laugh with his lips.

Dammit, I'm not going there. Instead, Jeb used his time more productively, adding up the implications of her words.

"You're on a second date," he said. "Something you've never taken lightly in your life. An old-fashioned gal like you is looking for marriage, not sex." He forced himself to the logical conclusion. "Do you want to marry Mike?"

She rolled her eyes. "Oddly enough, he didn't propose on our *first date.*"

"But that's what you're thinking," he persisted. "You want to get married, just like I do."

She busied herself finding salt and pepper, a napkin. "Okay, I admit I'd like to find a man who'll be a father to the kids. I'd like some company. And, um, a physical relationship." She was blushing again, as she fingered the locket Pat had given her on their first wedding anniversary. "But I'd like to point out I've made a considered decision—it's not an impulse reaction to a bump on the head."

"I told you, my head's fine," he said impatiently.

She handed him a jar of hot mustard, which he appreciated, since she considered his fondness for mustard with everything to be totally philistine.

"What do you mean, a considered decision?" he asked. "Either you want to get married, or you don't."

"There's married, and there's married," she said.

Not exactly helpful.

"Mom," Shane called from the living room, "Coach is coming up the walk."

"Here's my ride." Cara pulled silverware from the top drawer and handed it to Jeb. "Usual bedtimes for the kids." The instruction came with an eye roll that suggested he was incapable of getting the kids into bed on time.

Just because he hadn't done it before, didn't mean he couldn't tonight.

He needed a crash course in being father material. He had three kids to practice on, right here.

"I'm not sure when I'll be back," Cara said.

"I have an early start, so I'd appreciate if you're not too late." He might have given up on the idea of him and Cara, but damned if she was going to make out, or worse, with Mike on Jeb's watch.

She pulled a compact from her purse and applied a pinky-red lipstick. Which naturally made him want to kiss her again. Dammit, he'd gone years without thinking about her this much. Surely it couldn't all be one-sided?

"What do you think of this lipstick?" She pressed her lips together then pursed them. "Too pink?"

The truth hit Jeb: her talk about Mike's good looks, about her makeup…a woman would never discuss those things with a guy she was attracted to. Cara was talking to him as if…as if he was one of her *girlfriends*.

All this time, since Pat died, he'd been here for her, given her the comfort and support she needed. Being understanding, being a friend. He'd done it because he wanted to, not out of any ulterior motive. But any other woman would have had the good sense to recognize his potential as a husband and father by now.

Not Cara. He'd done such a good job of being a no-strings buddy, she was more likely to paint his toenails than she was to fall for him!

The thought could have been emasculating, if Jeb hadn't been a hundred percent secure in his manhood.

"The color's fine," he told her. "You go, I have a couple of calls to make."

Starting with one to his PR rep, Leah Gibbs. Leah

was a nice woman, a smart woman. There'd been a spark of attraction when they met that Jeb had chosen not to follow up—at the time, he'd had his hands full with a very toned Pilates instructor. Leah was the kind of woman he should consider for a permanent connection.

He pressed to dial her number. Cara would want to know if he was "in love" with Leah. He didn't consider that relevant. When Jeb found the right woman, love would grow out of the time they spent together.

It was like driving a stock car. The more you did it, the more you loved it.

Leah answered on the second ring, sounding breathless, as if she'd dived for the phone.

"About our meeting in the morning," Jeb said. "Let's make it breakfast. The Excelsior Room at the Getaway. That'll give us time to talk about more than just work."

When Leah accepted with obvious enthusiasm, he called the Getaway, Charlotte's most expensive hotel, and made a breakfast reservation. He followed that with a couple more calls.

By the time he put away his phone and dug into the mustard-coated fish pie, he'd made some satisfying progress toward his new dream.

CARA PUSHED her dessert plate aside, the plum cobbler only half eaten. Cobbler was one of her favorites, but tonight it didn't interest her. Maybe she should have ordered something more exotic—the hazelnut millefeuille with chocolate liqueur....

"Coffee?" Mike asked.

"No, thanks." She patted her stomach. "I need to get home soon."

Mike signaled the waiter for the check. He picked up his wineglass. "One last toast."

Half an inch of merlot remained in Cara's glass; she clinked it against his.

"To us," he said.

She smiled, and sipped. Throughout dinner, she'd been distracted by the memory of Jeb's odd behavior tonight.

He hadn't kissed her when he arrived, and he'd gone to ridiculous lengths to avoid zipping up her dress. As if he felt that by touching Cara, by kissing her even on the cheek, he would be unfaithful to this woman he wanted to marry.

Whoever she was.

Cara drained her wine.

Had he told the woman how he felt? Maybe even asked her to move into his house on the lake, into that enormous master bedroom with the double shower....

She quashed her rioting imagination as Mike signed the credit card slip and stood. He held out a hand. "Let's get you home, Cinderella."

She put her hand in his. He was a decent guy, good company. Great with kids. Conversation had flowed easily through dinner, they'd played footsie under the table and it had been nice.

She reminded herself of those facts as they pulled into her driveway. Mike was a good driver, too. He didn't have the kind of flair that, say, Jeb did, but his style made for a more comfortable ride.

She should invite him for coffee. If only to prove to Jeb that she didn't care if he found someone to marry.

She caught her breath. She *didn't* care, and she didn't have anything to prove. She would only invite Mike in if she wanted to.

Suddenly, she wasn't sure.

"I'll see you to the door," Mike said, taking the immediate pressure off.

The porch light was on, and so were the living room and family room lights. Darkness upstairs suggested the kids hadn't gone to bed yet. Knowing Jeb, they'd be playing some rambunctious game that would stop them falling asleep until the small hours.

On the porch, Mike stepped close to Cara.

Invite him in. "Would you like—I had a lovely time tonight," she said.

"Me, too." He smiled, and it made him look boyishly enthusiastic. He was such a nice guy.

He leaned in to kiss her, and Cara decided to meet him halfway.

He wrapped his arms around her. He wasn't the first man she'd kissed in her recent dating stint, but this was probably the most pleasant. He tasted minty—which reminded her, she must buy some extra-sensitive toothpaste for Shane, who'd been complaining of "tingly teeth." Maybe a visit to the dentist was in order....

She became aware of Mike trying to part her lips, and obligingly let him in. There, that wasn't too bad. Quite nice, really.

The porch light flickered—she needed to buy new bulbs, the one outside the back door had blown two weeks ago....

Don't be so rude, she chided herself. *Pay attention.* If she concentrated on Mike, she'd probably enjoy his kiss a lot more. Resolutely, she focused on her date, on the sensation of his mouth, his tongue. On the feel of his shoulders beneath her splayed fingers—Jeb was right, Mike was a little lanky—on the sensation of his hands, sliding down her back…

CHAPTER FIVE

SO FAR, Jeb would rate his evening at Cara's house a ten out of ten. The kids had accepted his "father material" persona with only minor complaints, he had a breakfast date lined up, and a couple of other interesting women on the horizon.

Once he'd started thinking about it, he'd remembered that Susie Edmonds, wife of NASCAR Sprint Cup Series driver Ben Edmonds, had mentioned she had a young cousin who was "just the woman for him," should he ever want to settle down. And Rue Larrabee at the Cut'N'Chat hairdressing salon had told Jeb she had a client, a gorgeous cordon bleu cook, who deserved a very special man.

He'd successfully followed up both leads.

Yep, he had his quest for a wife well under control, he thought, as he heard the tip-tap of Cara's high heels on the porch. When she didn't immediately come inside, he went to check on her—and realized just before he opened the door the likely reason for a delay.

He froze, hand on the doorknob. He didn't want to cramp her style. Did he?

Jeb peered through the peephole. Yep, as he'd

guessed, she was kissing her date good-night. He stepped back from the door.

Half a minute later, he stuck his eye to the peephole again. They were still at it, for Pete's sake! How long could a simple good-night kiss take?

He ignored the fact that he'd often lingered several minutes himself. This was ridiculous, she'd just seen the guy a few days ago.

While he watched, Mike's hands moved south.

Jeb flung the door open with the force of a minor gale.

Cara leaped out of Mike's arms, tomato-red. She tugged her blue silk dress straight. Mike muttered a curse.

"Evening, folks," Jeb said pleasantly.

Mike's eyes widened. "You're Jeb Stallworth." His annoyance evaporated, replaced by awe.

Jeb hooked his thumbs in his jeans and leaned against the doorjamb. "Didn't Cara tell you I was baby-sitting?" He narrowed his gaze on her.

"We had other things to talk about," she said.

"Mike Davis." Mike shook hands with Jeb. "Great drive at Daytona. Sorry about the crash."

"Thanks," Jeb said, without the twinkling smile he usually reserved for fans.

"Young Shane sure is a big admirer of yours," Mike said.

This time, Jeb did smile. "The feeling's mutual."

Mike laced his fingers through Cara's. "We should all go to a race together, sweetie, maybe fly somewhere and make a weekend of it."

Sweetie?

"Uh…" Cara said.

"You're in California this weekend, aren't you?" Mike asked Jeb.

"Yeah, but the race is a sell-out." Jeb eyed their linked hands. He had no idea if the race was sold out or not.

"Fulcrum Racing can sometimes get us passes," Cara said.

Pat and Jeb had raced on the same team. Dixon Rogers and Isabel Mortimer, the brother and sister who owned Fulcrum, were unstinting in their generosity to Pat's family.

Jeb shook his head. "Not this weekend. The team has a lot of guests."

What was wrong with him? Cara could go to a race with anyone she wanted—it made no difference to him. He'd moved on.

"Some other time, maybe," Cara told Mike. "I'll mention it to Dixon."

Jeb looked pointedly at his watch.

"No problem." Mike dropped a quick kiss on her lips. "I'll call you."

Jeb waited until the guy was off Cara's porch before he headed back inside. She followed him in. He closed the door with a firm click.

Cara glanced into the family room. "Where are the kids?"

"In bed, of course." They both knew there was no of course about it. "I made sure their chores got done," Jeb said casually. "I found the list on the fridge." He didn't mention that he'd completed Lucy's chores—feeding the cat and watering the plants in the sunroom—himself. That little sweetheart was a total con artist—Shane and Dylan had hooted with laughter to hear he'd fallen for her tummy-ache story.

"That's great." Cara didn't bother to hide her surprise, he observed.

Not father material.

"Lucy's wiggly tooth came out," he reported. "You'd better notify the tooth fairy."

"Will do." She smiled, drawing his attention to her smudged lipstick.

"Okay, I'd better go." Jeb glanced around for his keys. Oh, yeah, in the kitchen.

"You don't have time for coffee?" Their usual ritual.

He was tempted. He could picture her curled up on the couch next to him, yawning away, hair tousled. *Tousled by Mike.*

You've moved on, walk away.

"No, thanks." In the kitchen, he found his keys on the island.

"You're not flying to California tomorrow, are you?" she asked. "Is that why you have an early start?"

Jeb tossed his keys in the air, and caught them. "I have a date. A breakfast date."

CARA FOLLOWED JEB to the front door, biting down on the urge to ask who he was dating. And if he was meeting her at breakfast, or before. Like, right now. Was that why he was rushing away?

"Thanks for looking after the kids." She straightened the lone umbrella in the terra cotta pot used to store anything long, thin and outdoorsy: umbrellas, softball bats, sticks that could serve as laser swords in a space game.

"My pleasure." He sounded distant. He wanted to leave.

"I appreciate you getting them into bed on time. And overseeing the chores." It touched her that he'd taken her comments the other day to heart.

"As you said, no right-minded woman will marry me if I won't make a good dad," he reminded her. "I'm getting in some practice."

She bristled. "On *my* kids?"

"You're the one who complained I let them run riot. You should be pleased."

"I…I am," she said feebly. When she wanted to say *how dare you practice on my kids so you can impress some other woman?* Which would be totally unreasonable. "Of course, there's more to it than chores and bedtime," she pointed out.

"I'm still on the bottom rung of the parenting skills ladder—got it." The old Jeb humor gleamed in his eyes, and she found herself smiling at him.

"You do have a way with the kids," she admitted. "So maybe not quite the bottom rung."

He clutched his chest. "Flatterer."

She laughed, and it felt so good, laughing with him again.

His mouth softened out of that noncommittal line it had been in ever since he arrived that evening. "Now, I really do need to go." He reached for the door handle.

To her shock, she discovered she lacked the courage to kiss his cheek. Jeb, whom she must have kissed a thousand times.

"Enjoy your breakfast date," she said awkwardly.

She'd lost her stomach for the details…so, naturally, he decided to share. "It's with Leah."

"Your PR rep?"

"Yeah. Nice girl."

Leah was pretty—very pretty—and also smart. Plus, she was at least five years younger than Cara.

"Is she the one you want to marry?" Cara asked. "The one you said you've met?"

"*You* said that," he corrected. "I haven't seen Leah outside of work before."

"You do know she's a vegetarian?" Cara asked. Jeb was what she'd call assertively carnivorous.

Jeb recoiled. "But she could cook me a steak, right, even if she didn't eat it?"

Cara wrinkled her nose. "She's one of those animals-are-people-too campaigners. I'm not sure she'd even sit down at a table with meat on it."

"But I wanted bacon and eggs for breakfast," he complained.

She snickered.

"Damn," he muttered. "I can't cancel breakfast now, I'll just have to make sure Leah doesn't get the wrong idea."

"That's probably best," she agreed.

He leaned against the wall, as if he wasn't going anywhere. "You probably know the other women I have lined up, too."

"How many are there?" she asked, aghast.

"I told you I want to find someone. How can I do that if I don't date?"

She shook her head.

"I'm seeing Susie Edmonds's cousin for lunch to-morrow," he said.

"Rosemary? Rosalie?" She spotted a spiderweb in the corner behind him and swiped it away.

Jeb moved aside. "Rosalie," he confirmed. "She's a doctor."

"And very attractive," Cara encouraged him.

He squinted. "Why are you saying it like that?"

"Um…I'm hoping it'll make up for the fact she doesn't like motor racing?"

"Doesn't—*what?*"

Cara winced apologetically. "If it has wheels and an engine, she's bored witless."

He raked a hand through his hair. "Why would I want a woman who doesn't like NASCAR?"

"I'll bet Susie was hoping you'd convert her."

He straightened away from the wall. "I'll have to cancel. Okay, third time lucky. I have a dinner date next week. Rue Larrabee set me up with one of her clients, Lisa Holt. She's an elementary schoolteacher—and a NASCAR fan."

Cara started to laugh.

Jeb groaned. "Tell me."

"I know Lisa, she's Dylan's teacher."

"What's wrong with her?"

Cara's mirth grew. "She's left two men at the altar. She's a runaway bride." She snorted. "But she probably wouldn't jilt *you.*"

He made a sound of disgust, as his shoulders sagged. "It's not funny. I seriously want to find someone."

Cara tried to sober up, but a weird sense of relief

kept her giggling. "You'd better accept it might take time."

"Either that or I need help." His eyes narrowed. "*Your* help."

That did the trick. Her amusement evaporated. "Mine?" It came out a squeak.

His devilish smile said he was warming to his theme. "You know me better than anyone, and you know just about everyone in NASCAR. How about you write me a list of suitable women?"

"I don't know what you want!" Last time she looked, Jeb was dating models and actresses. None of them seemed to last more than about a day and a half.

"Someone normal. Someone like you, only more…" He scanned Cara from top to toe.

"Youthful?" she suggested silkily.

"I was going to say *reasonable*." He smirked. "Age doesn't matter. I'll give you a list of qualities—you're good with lists."

"No, thanks."

"She needs to like NASCAR and preferably understand it so I don't have to explain everything."

"That narrows it down to about five million women."

"Kids are okay, good, even."

"Ah, yes, your instant family plan," she murmured.

"It'd be nice if she's pretty. Smart's a must. What else?" he mused. "Good sense of humor."

"That's original. Did you think of trying the Internet?"

He hushed her with a finger to her lips. Cara froze.

He dropped his hand. "I want a woman whose head won't be turned by the NASCAR lifestyle, who likes me for who I am."

"Maybe you should hang out incognito in a used car lot." Casually, she brushed the back of her hand across her lips to get rid of the tingling. "See who you can pick up."

"Cute," he said, looking at her lips. "Not. Come on, honey, help me out here."

Oh, no, she knew that cajoling smile. She stepped past him and opened the door for him to leave. "I refuse to believe you need my help getting a girlfriend."

He didn't budge. "Damn right I don't. All I want is a list of qualified names. I'll take it from there." He winked. "Consider it a token of your gratitude for my babysitting."

A chill breeze wafted through the open door. Cara shivered. Jeb didn't need to remind her of the million things he'd done for her over the past few years—most important of which had been making her smile through difficult times. And wasn't this what she wanted—Jeb being his old, relaxed self with her? Being her buddy? This was surely the least she could do for him.

"Fine," she said. "I'll write a list."

"You can bring it to Maudie's tomorrow."

They knew each other so well, their routines had begun to collide. Jeb and some of his crew ate at Maudie's Diner most Thursdays, before the pandemonium of race weekend kicked in. Cara had gotten into the habit of purchasing a takeout meal from Maudie's that day. She and Jeb usually had iced tea while she waited for her meal and he for his team.

"I might need more time."

"You can do it," he said confidently. "By the way, I thought of one more essential quality."

She sighed. "Yes?"

"Chemistry."

He was outrageous!

"How am I supposed to figure out whether you'll have chemistry with someone?" she demanded.

"You're smart, use your imagination."

He hooked his thumbs in his jeans, clearly enjoying her discomfort. But she wasn't beaten. "Isn't it time you left?" she asked sweetly. "You have a date with a tofu omelet in the morning."

He shuddered. "Touché."

She stepped aside to let him depart, but he moved the same way and they bumped. Automatically, Jeb steadied her, his hands strong around her upper arms.

"Thanks." Cara sounded breathless. She looked up at him, ready to laugh it off. But when she met his brown eyes, something flooded her body. Heat, light…*helium?* She felt weightless, as if she might float away without the grip of his hands holding her in place.

I shouldn't have finished that merlot.

"Well, good night." She shoved the door in his direction so that it bumped his shoe.

Jeb released her. "See you at Maudie's. Bring the list."

Then he was gone. Reversing down her driveway in his sports car, glancing over his shoulder so she couldn't see his face.

Cara closed the door, then leaned against it. Thank goodness that was over. How had a simple date with Mike ended up so complicated?

Typical of Jeb to turn something most people did

logically—like finding a spouse—into fun and games. Fun for him, at least.

She was the one who had to dream up a list of women he could chase after.

Cara's mind blanked.

CHAPTER SIX

CARA TOOK A DEEP, appreciative sniff of the aroma of home cooking as she approached the chrome-trimmed counter at Maudie's. The pink neon Maudie's Down Home Diner sign flickered on the baby-blue wall behind.

"Hey, it's Wonder Nurse." Sheila Trueblood, pocket-size owner of Maudie's, greeted her with a wave. "Lasagna to go?"

Cara considered changing her order, just to disprove Jeb's point about her being set in her ways. But Jeb wasn't here yet, and she liked the lasagna.

"Yes, please, make it extra large." She sank onto a bar stool, red vinyl trimmed with chrome to match the counter. "And do you have any lemon-meringue pie? I have three starving kids at home, and nothing in the fridge."

"Emergency rations, our specialty. Pie's still in the oven, it might be a few minutes." Sheila called out the order to the cook. Then she came around the counter and hugged Cara. "Tea? I assume Jeb is joining you?"

"So I believe." Cara fished her wallet out of her handbag. She paid Sheila, then added extra sugar to both glasses of iced tea that the other woman slid across the counter.

The door opened behind her, and she turned, her hands suddenly clammy on the tea glasses, expecting to see Jeb. But it was Bart Branch, another NASCAR Sprint Cup Series driver. At least, she assumed it was Bart. She didn't know him well, and his identical twin Will was also a race driver. But Will was married, so less likely to be buying his dinner at Maudie's, Cara assumed. She nodded a greeting to him.

"Be with you in a minute, hon," Sheila called to Bart. Then, to Cara, "Any chance you'll join us for Tarts next week?"

"Uh, not sure." The Tuesday Tarts were a group of women, most of them involved in NASCAR, who met on Tuesday nights in the back room at Maudie's. Rue Larrabee from the Cut'N'Chat had started the group years ago, with Maudie's former owner providing the venue. Sheila had embraced the tradition when she took over the diner. Once a regular participant, Cara had attended sporadically since Pat died.

"You know you miss us," Sheila said.

"I do," she agreed, hit by a pang of nostalgia for the camaraderie of the NASCAR world. After she'd recovered from the strangeness of Jeb's request last night, she'd enjoyed recalling all of the people she knew in the sport—though she'd tried to focus on single women. It was by her own choice, or at least her own apathy, that she was no longer much involved.

"I'll come," she announced. "I'd love to see the girls again."

"Attagirl." Sheila patted her shoulder. "Now we just need to get you to a few races."

Cara kept up with the NASCAR Sprint Cup Series

on TV, but she hadn't been to a live race since the last one in Charlotte. "You're right, the kids are always hounding me to go."

"How are those adorable bambinos of yours?" Sheila wiped the already immaculate counter. She was one of those people who never stopped working, even when all the work was done.

"They're fine. Doesn't that thing give you a headache?" Cara pointed at the wavering neon light.

Sheila tsked. "It's been putting out more heat than usual, I think it's on its last legs. But it costs a fortune to replace. I'll wait until it drives me insane."

Cara smiled. Sheila must make a very comfortable living out of Maudie's, with so many NASCAR teams frequenting the place. Yet though she was generous to a fault with anyone who needed help, when it came to controlling the costs of her business, she was a total Scrooge.

"I'll take the tea over there." Cara indicated the booth where she usually sat with Jeb. "Or I'll be seeing pink flashing neon in my dreams."

As she turned, the door opened again. Once more, it wasn't Jeb. Cara let out a breath. This was ridiculous, feeling so nervous about seeing her old friend.

The new arrival was a young woman, whose short, dark hair emphasized her fine-boned features and wide brown eyes. At first glance, she barely looked older than the toddler clinging to her hand, but as she approached, Cara realized she had to be nineteen or twenty. The toddler didn't have her mom's coloring— her curly hair was lighter and she was chubby. Well looked-after, in Cara's professional opinion.

"Help you, hon?" Sheila's usual welcoming smile was tinged with concern.

Cara knew why. The young woman looked exhausted.

The young mother blinked. "Uh, yeah, we need to eat."

The child tugged on her hand. She wore no wedding ring, Cara observed.

"Lily, sweetie, just a minute." Her tone was loving, but tired. She glanced back at Sheila. "My name's Mellie Donovan. I'm looking for a job. The sign in your window says Help Wanted."

"First things first," Sheila said. "Let's get you fed, Mellie Donovan, then when I'm convinced you can stand up for more than five minutes, we'll talk about work." She handed over a menu. "The kids' food—nuggets and stuff—is at the bottom left. Take a seat anywhere you like, and I'll come take your order."

Mellie accepted the menu. "Why don't you choose us a table by the window, Lily?" she suggested.

The toddler headed toward the booths at a waddling run, arms outstretched.

"Slowly," Mellie called…just as Lily crashed into a chair and fell over.

Her jaw fell open with shock that Cara knew would turn to tears. Sure enough, Lily drew in an enormous breath, ready to squawk. But before any sound could emerge, Bart Branch reached out from his booth and swept her up.

"Hey, little lady, did you just smack that chair?" he teased as he got to his feet.

The child stared at him, distracted from her fall.

"You gotta go easy on Sheila's furniture with those big muscles of yours." He touched one pudgy arm.

Cara smiled. Bart's nonsense had Lily prettily confused. One tiny finger prodded Bart's left nostril.

"Lily, come here." Mellie held out her hands for the child. "Thanks for your help, I'll take her now." She sounded wary, as any mom would when a strange man picked up her daughter.

"This is Bart Branch, honey," Sheila called. "You don't need to worry about him."

Mellie didn't react to the name. Which implied she wasn't one of the star-struck NASCAR fans who'd heard that drivers sometimes hung out at Maudie's. A point in her favor, if Sheila was serious about employing her.

"Could you give her back, please?" Mellie asked politely.

Bart was eyeing her with interest, no doubt intrigued by the lack of recognition. "Sure," he said in the deep drawl that attracted women by the score. "You have a cute daughter."

He passed Lily over, and there was a moment of jostling, when he and Mellie both had their hands on the child.

Cara saw it: the fraction of a second when they froze, fingers overlapping. Then Mellie tugged Lily away.

Bart didn't step back, just stood looking down at Mellie, whose color was high. He cleared his throat, but didn't speak.

Bart was attracted to Mellie, Cara realized. At a different level from his famed flirtatiousness, if his speechless state was any indication. Could one brief, almost accidental touch do that?

Jeb had mentioned *chemistry*. Was this what he meant? How was Cara supposed to predict who he'd have chemistry with?

Then Mellie turned away, carried Lily to a booth. Bart sat down again, and it was as if the whole thing had never happened.

Cara resumed her progress toward her booth. Jeb walked in before she got halfway across the diner.

"Hey, Sheila." He took both glasses from Cara.

She noticed he didn't kiss her cheek. Maybe things weren't quite right between them yet.

"How was work?" he asked, as she slid into the booth opposite him.

"I had eight births—mothers and babies all well."

Jeb whistled.

"How about you?"

"Breakfast with Leah, then I stopped by a fast-food joint for a bacon biscuit. Man, there's no way I could give up that stuff." He patted his stomach with remembered satisfaction. "Then the doctor checked up on my wrist, I watched replays of previous races at California, and had a progress meeting with Secure Communications." Secure Communications was Jeb's primary sponsor. He stirred his tea. "So, where's my list?"

"I don't have it."

"Busy day," he said understandingly.

She nodded, though it wasn't the whole truth. During any labor there were times when she was free to let her thoughts wander. But today her mind had stayed firmly away from eligible women for Jeb. *Must try harder.*

"Maybe tomorrow?" he said.

"You have a one-track mind," she accused.

"When I make a decision, I like to move ahead. It's no different from what you're doing with your dates."

"I didn't ask you to find my next husband for me," she pointed out.

He snorted. "Yeah, well, I sure wouldn't have chosen Mike."

"He's very—"

"Nice," Jeb said at the same time she did. Only when he said it, it didn't sound like a compliment.

"He's the kind of man I'm looking for."

Another snort.

"Who would you have recommended?" she asked, goaded.

He eyed her for so long that she started to squirm. She was overly conscious that her T-shirt was a little tight; her breathing constricted.

At last, he spoke. "I can tell you, it wouldn't be anyone like Mike, my cautious Cara." He reached across and brushed a knuckle across her chin.

Instinctively, she knocked his hand away.

The violence of the movement startled them both. They stared at each other, and tension crackled.

Jeb opened his mouth. His lips—*dammit, this is not about Jeb's lips!*

He was looking at her mouth, too.

"Cancel that, I don't want to know," Cara said quickly.

"Hey, you two." Ryder McGraw, Jeb's crew chief, appeared next to the table. With him were Paul Amos, the team's car chief, and Todd Thompson, one of the mechanics. They squeezed into the booth, Ryder snagging a chair from an adjacent table to go at the end. All four men ordered burgers and fries from Sheila, along with iced teas.

"Cara, how are the kids doing?" Ryder shifted the ketchup bottle to make more room in front of him.

Filling him in about her family led to a discussion of mutual acquaintances. When the food arrived, Ryder offered her his fries; Cara took a couple.

"Car looking good?" she asked. Because polite though Ryder was to engage in social chat with her, she knew all these men had the race car on their minds.

The lack of enthusiasm in their responses suggested there had been problems preparing the No. 464 car.

"If anyone can pull a rabbit out of the hat on race day, it's you guys," she comforted them.

Ryder grinned. "That's my motto. The beautiful woman is always right."

"You look tired, Cara," Jeb said abruptly, as he squeezed mustard over his burger.

Thanks a lot. She wondered if he'd paid Leah the same compliment during their breakfast date. "Like I said, it's been a long day."

"You look great," Ryder reassured her.

The conversation turned back to the race car. Cara didn't follow most of the technicalities, but she enjoyed listening to the to-and-fro between men who loved their jobs. When you weren't personally responsible for producing a winning race car, it was a unique form of relaxation. She'd missed it.

But throughout, she was conscious of Jeb opposite her, his forearms resting on the table between bites of burger. She fidgeted in her seat, and her knee brushed his.

His gaze flickered in her direction, then away again.

Unfortunately, she couldn't ignore the contact as easily, a realization that alarmed her. She stilled, not wanting to touch him again.

Sheila came over to top off the tea. "Your food will be out in two minutes," she told Cara.

"Great." Cara put a hand over her glass to refuse the top-off. She reached beneath the table for her purse.

"Bring that list next time," Jeb said.

She glared; she'd managed to forget that little task for a few minutes. "Or you could just find your own dates."

Her comment generated a lot of interest from the guys around the table. When Jeb didn't rise to their provocation, Cara fueled the fire.

"I'm sure Ryder doesn't need any help getting a woman," she continued. Then realized how that sounded. As if she found Jeb's crew chief attractive.

Well, he was. With his dark hair and broad shoulders he looked a little like Jeb. Not as handsome, of course… Although right now, with Ryder grinning at her as if he'd just won the lottery, in stark contrast with Jeb's scowl, he looked very appealing. She smiled back.

"So you're fixing Jeb up," he said speculatively. "Interesting."

"How's that?" she asked.

"I always suspected there was something going on between you two." His glance encompassed her and Jeb.

"No way," Jeb said emphatically.

His eagerness to dispel the idea was insulting.

"Definitely not," Cara chipped in. "I've been seeing my son's soccer coach."

Ryder looked…disappointed? Her mind replayed his words and actions tonight. Sharing his fries with her, calling her a beautiful woman, reassuring her she didn't look tired. And now, that warm regret in his eyes.

Was he interested in her?

"It's nothing serious with the coach," she told Ryder.

Because now that she thought about it, the crew chief was much more her kind of guy than Mike.

Maybe that was why she hadn't thrilled to Mike's kiss. Ryder was part of the world she loved: NASCAR, with all its intricacies and excitement. She'd stayed away in recent times because there were too many reminders of Pat and what she'd lost. But that didn't change the fact that NASCAR was home.

Maybe she should look closer to home for someone to share her life. NASCAR was full of men who knew about Pat and respected his memory. Who could accept that she had firm ideas about what she wanted from a remarriage.

She attempted a dazzling smile at Ryder. He straightened in his seat, then leaned in to her.

"So, you're unattached?" he asked, his voice deeper than it had been a moment ago.

"Absolutely," she said.

Ryder sat back, his expression calculating. "In that case, how about dinner Sunday night?"

"You'll be in California," she reminded him.

"That's what I mean, dinner in California." He grinned. "You and the kids could come to the race."

Her pulse quickened at the thought of being back in

the buzz of the race track. "It seems a little short notice. I'm not working this weekend, but there'd be so many arrangements…"

"You can fly up on Dixon's plane on Saturday morning." Ryder generously offered his boss's services as chauffeur. "You'd stay in my motor home—I'll bunk in with Jeb, if he'll have me. We'll go out for dinner after the race. We're all staying on for a sponsor party, where I need to put in an appearance, but after that we can find a nice restaurant. I'll even organize a sitter for the kids."

Jeb bit into his burger, his blank expression communicating his lack of interest in her dating arrangements. Yet he expected her to devote herself to his!

"I'd love to come to the race," she told Ryder. "But aren't all the guest passes already allocated?"

Ryder frowned. "I don't think so. Let me check." He pulled out his cell, called Dixon. When he'd finished he said, "No problem, plenty of passes available. Dixon's thrilled to have you and the kids on his plane and at the track."

Cara slanted a glance at Jeb, who gazed impassively back. So, what, he'd lied to Mike, just because he thought he was too *nice?* All that showed was how screwed up Jeb was.

"Thanks, Ryder, I'm excited already—" did Jeb just snort? "—and I know the kids will be, too." She spotted Sheila, waving out. "Looks like my meal's ready."

"Dixon's secretary will call you tomorrow about travel arrangements," Ryder said.

Paul Amos stood to let Cara out of the booth.

"See y'all on the weekend," she said happily.

Three of the men said goodbye.

Jeb said, "By the way, honey, that extra quality we were talking about last night?"

Chemistry.

"I think we managed to identify it," he said.

That moment before Ryder arrived, when she'd overreacted to Jeb's touch.

That wasn't chemistry, that was…something else.

"I'll get that list to you in California," she promised. And meant it.

CHAPTER SEVEN

"MOM, JEB'S TAKING ME to watch him practice, okay?" Dylan barely drew breath as he grabbed a ball cap emblazoned with the Secure Communications logo, then raced out of the motor home.

"That's fine," Cara called after him. "Stay out of the way of any cars being pushed around." Like he was listening. She rolled her eyes. "Are you girls ready for some lemonade?"

They'd only been at the track eight hours, but Lucy had already made friends with Bella, daughter of Grace Clark, who'd recently married the reigning NASCAR Sprint Cup Series champion, Garrett Clark.

Bella had invited herself to Ryder's motor home for a play-date, and now the girls were using Shane's model race car collection as "people" in a game they'd invented. Shane was playing soccer with a bunch of boys his age, so hopefully he wouldn't discover the abuse of his precious collection.

"Yes, please, Mama," Lucy said.

Cara poured the drinks and summoned the girls to the table.

Lucy sighed with satisfaction as she stirred the ice cubes in her glass. "I like NASCAR."

"You should come to next week's race," Bella said authoritatively. "My new dad says Las Vegas is the best track. My new dad is cool."

"Can we, Mama?" Lucy asked. "Can we come back next week?"

"The race isn't here next week, sweetheart," Cara prevaricated. "As Bella says, it's in Las Vegas."

She was loving being at the track, in the bosom of NASCAR. So far today, she'd lunched with a bunch of women, including her old acquaintance Patsy Grosso, co-owner with her husband, Dean, of Cargill-Grosso Racing. Then she'd had coffee with Sandra Taney—Sandra and her husband, who owned Taney Motorsports, had recently had their first baby, a little boy named Brandon. Cara knew Sandra from way back as a seriously dynamic PR company owner, so it was fun to see her relaxed and cooing over her son.

Everyone was so friendly, so welcoming. A woman Cara had never met before had insisted on lending her a dress for the sponsor party after the race, after Cara expressed her dissatisfaction with the outfit she'd brought with her. The woman, Becky Peters, was engaged to Jake McMasters, a distant cousin of Patsy's—she and Jake were staying in the Grossos' motor home this weekend. Becky, a model, had assured Cara she always traveled with excess clothing. When she'd produced a Vera Wang cocktail dress, Cara had abandoned all thought of turning down her generous offer.

That was NASCAR for you—a sport that bound families, friends and even strangers together.

Cara glanced at her watch. Ryder had invited her to the pits to watch Jeb's practice. "Girls, I'm going to take you to Bella's nana's place in fifteen minutes, so when you've finished your drinks you need to clear away that mess."

"Nana" was Patsy Grosso. Grace Clark had recently discovered she was Patsy and Dean's daughter, Gina, stolen from a Nashville hospital soon after her birth. Her reunion with her famous parents had made headlines around the world…and transformed the lives of the Grosso family.

After she'd handed the girls over to Patsy, Cara wandered to the garage, enjoying the contrast between the balmy California air and Charlotte's chill this morning.

Ryder saw her from a distance and waved. Although he was busy, he'd been the perfect blend of gentleman and enthusiastic date since she arrived. Hopefully, when they had a chance to spend some time alone, the chemistry between them might build. Because right now, it did feel a little flat. After the race, Cara told herself, when they went to dinner, that was the time to figure out Ryder's dating potential.

The No. 464 car was being given a final once-over by the team mechanics. Jeb stood to one side, talking to Leah, his publicist. Who was acting decidedly unprofessionally, Cara observed. Did she need to lean into Jeb that way? She was practically batting her eyelashes. Obviously he hadn't been clear enough about his life membership of Carnivores Anonymous.

Cara dragged her eyes away…and noticed a group of fans zeroing in on Jeb. All women, all blonde and gorgeous, but not in a cookie-cutter way.

"Jeb," one of them called.

Jeb wouldn't have been a red-blooded man if his face

hadn't lit with interest when he caught sight of the talent headed his direction. "Hey, ladies, what can I do for you?"

They needed no further encouragement. A burst of chatter broke out as they swarmed him, asking for autographs, taking photos.

Behind them, Cara noticed, was another group of women, waiting their turn with ill-disguised impatience. Where had they all come from? It wasn't even race day.

Pat had had his share of female admirers, but though he'd been male enough to notice the attention, he'd never had eyes for anyone but Cara.

Jeb had no reason for self-restraint. He was single. Available.

"Overwhelming, aren't they?" Ryder said beside her.

She turned to him with relief. "Is it always like this?"

"Pretty much." He eyed her quizzically. "Didn't you know?"

"I guess…I didn't realize women found Jeb that attractive. At least, not so many of them."

Ryder guffawed, and the sound caught Jeb's attention. He grinned at his crew chief. One of the fans sighed audibly at the sight of that smile.

"They're all so gorgeous," Cara said. *And young.* "Is there a plastic surgery tent here that I missed?"

He laughed again. "Don't tell me those chickadees make you feel insecure."

"Not really." She tugged down her long-sleeved T-shirt, aware that if any midriff showed it would be far from toned. She was reasonably fit, but after three kids…

"You're way more interesting than them," Ryder said.

Cara's ego re-inflated slightly.

"I'm looking forward to our dinner tomorrow," he continued. "Shame we can't do it tonight, but Saturday night's our last chance to cement our teamwork ahead of the race, and we always do that over a meal."

"Tomorrow's fine."

The car chief called out to Ryder, and he excused himself.

She stood for a moment, watching Jeb greet the new batch of women. She felt…excluded. *All I have to do is walk over and say hello. He's my friend.*

She put the thought into action, walked right up to him as if she owned him. "Hi," she said.

"Hey." Did his face soften? "If you're looking for Dylan, he's over by the hauler, helping Tony grill burgers."

A race team was always hungry, and if the hauler driver was handy with a grill, it kept everyone happy.

"I'm looking for you," she said. In the face of her obvious confidence, the other women melted away.

Something flared in his eyes.

Cara dug into the pocket of her jeans and pulled out a folded piece of paper. "This is yours."

He opened it. His head jerked up. "My list."

"You asked for it."

He scanned the handwritten names. "You even provided phone numbers."

"What are friends for?"

"I've met her." He pointed to the first name. "You're right, she has definite potential." He read on. "Who's Emma-Lee Dalton?"

"Gil Sizemore's PA. I don't know her personally, but one of her sisters is married to Adam Sanford, the other to Roberto Castillo. The whole family is nuts about NASCAR."

"Oh, yeah, blonde girl. Very cute," he approved.

Cara smiled stiffly.

He moved down the list. "She's good. Yep, and her." He quirked an eyebrow. "You've worked hard."

"As you said, lists are my forte." So why, the further he read down the list, did she feel more and more of a loser?

"Thanks." He leaned forward as if he might kiss her cheek, then stopped. "Want to grab a burger?"

"Sure." She fought the urge to gloat at the fans as they left.

Just as well, because outside the garage, there were more fans gawping at Jeb.

"You seem very popular," she observed.

"No more than any other driver," he said, amused.

She doubted that. Cara could have been invisible, so consuming was the women's interest in Jeb. Besides, much as she'd adored Pat, she had to admit that Jeb was more…eye-catching. "You could date a different girl every night."

"I could," he agreed, and something turned cold in the pit of her stomach. "But that's not what I want, remember?"

Her hand bumped against Jeb's, sending a jolt through her. He slanted her a sidelong look, and she read his silent message: *Chemistry.*

"Mom, I'm cooking the burgers," Dylan shouted as they approached. He was indeed standing behind the grill, tongs at the ready. Burger patties sizzled in front of him. As Cara watched, a tongue of flame shot through the bars of the grill.

She sped up to a trot. Only to find Jeb's hand on her arm. He didn't let her shake him off.

"I ran through the safety drill with him earlier," Jeb said. "If the flames get out of control he knows to turn off the gas at the bottle, rather than get too close to the grill. You'll notice his ball cap completely covers his hair, and that glove he's wearing is flame retardant— he thought it was nerdy until I reminded him that NASCAR drivers wear fireproof gloves."

Cara's jaw dropped. "You thought of all that?"

"Hell, no." He laughed. "I've been watching you run through these drills for years. I know them by heart."

She colored. "You make me sound paranoid. Or like a sergeant-major."

"You mainly manage to do it in a way that the kids don't realize they're being supervised to within an inch of their lives," he assured her.

Clearly she didn't fool him, though. "It's just…I worry."

"I know. I think it's cute—at least, when it's about the kids." He caught a strand of hair that had escaped her ponytail in his fingers, then dropped it.

"Thank you." Oops, it sounded as if she was thanking him for touching her hair. "For Dylan. For watching out for him," she babbled, flustered.

They'd reached the grill. A surreptitious glance told her Jeb was right. Dylan was well-protected.

"These smell delicious," she announced.

Her proud son slapped a burger pattie between two halves of a bun like a pro, then added onion, a slice of tomato and a couple of shreds of lettuce. He handed the assembled burger to her along with a paper napkin.

Cara waited while Dylan served Jeb. She saw the affinity between them, and couldn't help noticing the strength inherent in Jeb's jaw, the respect Dylan instinctively accorded him. Had she been too hasty telling Jeb he wasn't father material?

Jeb joined her, and they bit into their burgers together. Juices spurted down Cara's chin.

"Let me get that." Jeb held out his napkin.

Annoyingly ruffled at the prospect of his touch, she beat him to it, scrubbed at her face with her own napkin. Watching, he smiled, and when her eyes met his, she felt the connection as a zap of electricity.

Oh, no. Cara ducked her head, stared unseeingly down at her burger. Jeb was right. There was chemistry galore between them, and somehow she'd only just figured that out.

I'm attracted to Jeb. Just like when I first met him.

Only now, she knew exactly where attraction could take two people, and how tempting that destination was.

Briefly, she tried convincing herself that Jeb wasn't remotely her kind of guy. But she only had to look at the effort he'd made with her kids the past few days to start questioning her reliance on her old assumptions about him.

Suddenly, she wished she hadn't given Jeb that list. Wished she wasn't here in California as Ryder's date.

If she thought there was any chance at all Jeb could be the man for her, she had to move fast.

CHAPTER EIGHT

JEB HAD QUALIFIED eighth for the race, and now he was sandwiched between Kent Grosso and Zack Matheson—two top drivers who'd be hard to get away from.

He liked this track, liked the smooth surface and the mild banking. He wasn't the only driver to consider California one of his favorites, but he had more reason to than most. He'd won here twice, and had never finished lower than tenth.

He wasn't about to blow that record. But he needed to get past Matheson.

"Grosso's buddy is about to join him," his spotter said, signaling that Roberto Castillo, the other driver on the Cargill-Grosso team, was catching up to Kent.

"Gotcha." Jeb wondered what strategy Kent and Roberto had in mind. Whatever it was, it would be good. He should make his move before Roberto got here.

It was tight, but when Matheson ran higher than usual in Turn One, Jeb stole the pass. His spotter allowed himself a brief whoop before he resumed his normal emotionless commentary.

"Keep it up, Jeb," Ryder said through the earpiece.

In that moment, driving this perfectly set-up car and with their race strategy playing out with balletic precision, Jeb could almost forgive him for dating Cara.

Don't think about her. Determined to exorcise her from his thoughts, Jeb threw the car into Turn Three, fueled by speed-lust, competitiveness and, dammit, plain old jealousy. If he didn't need Ryder's top-notch skills, he'd trade crew chiefs in a heartbeat. Where did the guy get off, inviting Cara to the race?

"Easy, buddy," Ryder said into his earpiece. For a second, Jeb thought he might have spoken out loud. Then he realized Ryder was referring to his driving.

"Car's loose," he said sourly.

"Driver's uptight," Ryder said calmly.

Damn wiseass crew chief.

The wall loomed too close and Jeb focused on his steering. What was it to him if Cara dated Ryder? Jeb's job was to win the race. He could do with a victory after that crash at Daytona, not to mention a couple of late-season smashes last year.

After the race, he'd call the first woman on Cara's list.

He spent the closing laps vying for position with Justin Murphy, his teammate, and Garrett Clark. Twice, Clark passed him. Once, Murphy did. Each time, Jeb managed to snatch the lead back.

The three cars were so close. The crowd was on its feet.

They roared as Jeb passed the checkered flag in first place.

I hope Cara's watching.

He ran a victory lap, spinning the occasional doughnut, then headed to Victory Lane. He hauled himself through the window opening and jumped down. As he removed his helmet, people slapped his back, called their congratulations.

At last, Jeb's head was out of the helmet. The first person he saw was Cara, right in front of him, with the kids.

"You were wonderful." She sounded odd, shy almost.

"Thanks." In that moment, he felt wonderful. The kids grabbed on to his legs, whooping their delight, but Jeb barely registered the noise.

He had to kiss Cara. *I shouldn't.*

He'd earned it. *I'm moving on from her.*

It would be positively wrong not to celebrate his victory with a kiss. *Ah, what the hell. What harm can it do? I'll move on tomorrow.*

Jeb bent his head to hers.

Their mouths met.

Flashes of memory, of that kiss long ago. Of a darkened doorway, of the haunting twang of a country ballad, of sweet, young lips beneath his.

Chemistry. In super-size quantities.

Damn.

Jeb pulled back and let Ryder steer him toward the press.

"Justin came in second," Ryder told him, not sounding as thrilled as he ought to. Oh, yeah, Jeb had just kissed his date.

"Fantastic." Jeb couldn't remember the last time the team had had a one-two finish. "We'll be celebrating tonight."

"Yeah." But there was a tiny hesitation before Ryder spoke. What was that about? Then Jeb figured it out.

"The sponsor will be all over you at the party," he said with satisfaction.

"It's the drivers they really want," Ryder said.

"The CEO of Secure Communications loves you," Jeb reminded him. "When he signed on, he made it clear he was going for the package—driver plus crew chief."

Ryder's grunt lacked enthusiasm.

"The guys will want a piece of you, too." Jeb laid it on thick. "You're their inspiration, and today they had the payoff."

Ryder stopped. "You don't have a problem with me dating Cara, do you?"

Jeb took the opportunity to reply to a fan's congratulations, shouted from the other side of the fence. Which enabled him to ignore the question.

Ryder waited patiently. "There'll be other dinners," he warned.

Jeb should say *Of course there will,* and wish his crew chief well.

He couldn't do it.

CARA'S STOMACH FLUTTERED as she slid the butterfly onto the pin of her diamond earring. The fluttering wasn't because she was going out for dinner with Ryder. He'd told her after the race he'd have to spend the entire evening at the party, celebrating the team's superb finishes appropriately. He'd probably be too busy to spend much time with her. Of course, she understood.

So now she was wearing the amethyst satin Vera Wang dress Becky Peters had lent her, doing a more attentive job of her makeup than usual, and fluttering for…who?

"You look pretty, Mama," Shane said.

There you go, for her kids. She dropped a kiss on his hair. "Thanks, sweetie. You guys ready?"

Jeb's motor home driver, a short, buxom woman named Sally, had arrived to babysit Lucy. But Shane and Dylan both had Dixon Rogers's permission to attend the first hour or so of the party. Cara had never seen them clean up so fast or take such care brushing their teeth and hair.

"Yep." Dylan answered for his brother and himself. He was almost beside himself with excitement—to him, Justin Murphy was a mysterious quantity, one he couldn't wait to investigate.

A knock sounded at the motor home door. "That'll be Mr. McGraw," she said. "Can you get it, Dylan?"

He didn't need asking twice; he had the door open before Cara had finished talking.

"Mom, it's Uncle Jeb."

Cara's other earring clattered into the sink; she managed to grab it just before it disappeared down the plughole. Her hands shook slightly as she pushed the earring through her ear. She checked her face in the mirror one last time, and was more or less satisfied she looked her best.

She exited the tiny bathroom. "Hi, Jeb."

He opened his mouth, then closed it again. And stared.

Cara touched the corners of her mouth—she'd

snacked on the kids' pizza earlier, did she have sauce on her face?

Shane said smugly, "Doesn't Mama look pretty?"

Poor Jeb, backed into a corner by her loving son. Doubtless he saw far prettier women all the time. Cara would never again look like one of those girls who'd been all over Jeb earlier—if she ever had.

"You don't have to answer that," she told him. Awkward, she ran her hands over her hips, saw his gaze follow the movement. She let her hands drop.

Jeb cleared his throat. "I think the word you're looking for, Shane, is *incredible*." Only he wasn't looking at Shane. He was looking at Cara.

"Thanks. You look nice, too."

Although he wore nothing fancier than dress jeans and a striped shirt, *incredible* was also the right word to describe him. Where his shirt was open at the throat it was clear he was tanned even in winter, and his dark hair had that hint of unruliness that said *this guy makes his own rules*.

"Where's Ryder?" she asked belatedly.

"He had to meet with an official from NASCAR, something about one of our guys misbehaving. I told him I'd walk you all over to the party."

The boys needed no further invitation; they were out the door and hanging on to Jeb.

"I hope this won't inconvenience your date," she said, fishing.

"I don't have a date," he said with a mock forlornness that made Dylan giggle.

Cara smiled. "I'm surprised you haven't called half that list by now."

Jeb didn't reply. Did that mean he *had* called the women on the list? If so…

She began a brisk walk through the motor home lot, thinking all the way.

THE PARTY WAS HELD in one of the sponsor suites lining pit road. The room was already filling up when Cara arrived, but she saw Ryder immediately. He must have managed to wrap up his meeting.

"You look great." He kissed her cheek.

"Thanks." She tried not to compare his *great* unfavorably with Jeb's *incredible*. Ryder looked very nice, too, with dark hair neatly groomed, a white shirt and dress jeans.

He handed her a glass of champagne, then asked the kids what they'd like. See, he was a nice guy, just like Jeb.

Of course, no one was quite like Jeb. She watched as he greeted the wife of the Secure Communications CEO with his famous smile. Then he was caught up in other introductions, to men wanting to rehash the race and women who were mainly content just to look.

She swigged her champagne, let the bubbles soothe her throat.

"Let me introduce you to some of the sponsors." Ryder took her elbow and steered her toward the bar, where a cluster of middle-aged men and their wives stood chatting.

Now, this she knew. She'd had years of chatting to Pat's sponsors. She launched into the conversation and it was as if she'd never been away.

"You were brilliant with those guys," Ryder said,

leaning on the bar after the guests made for the buffet. "But I'd rather it was just you and me, in a restaurant." The glint in his eye was too proprietary for Cara's liking.

"I'm really enjoying being with *everyone*," she said. The emphasis was none too subtle; and Ryder was well-known for being one of the smartest crew chiefs in the sport.

"Ah," he said. "I see."

"You're a great guy," she began.

He held up a hand. "No explanation necessary. It was worth a try, but no hearts were broken in the course of the experiment."

She laughed, grateful for his attitude.

"Still friends?" he asked.

"Of course." She patted his hand, resting on the bar. Doing so, she caught a glimpse of his watch. "Nine o'clock! The boys should be in bed by now."

She scanned the room, and eventually saw Shane's foot sticking out from beneath a tablecloth. She crouched down and lifted the cloth. Dylan, Shane and another kid were playing a card game under the table.

She pounced on Shane from behind; he squawked with fake horror. "Bedtime," she said.

"Aw, Mom." Dylan started in on the groaning, but she stuck to her guns.

The kids wanted to say good-night to Jeb, and she also sent them to see Ryder. At last, they made it outside. It was dark, but streetlamps provided sufficient light to see their way home.

By the time she'd handed the boys over to the sitter, Cara was of two minds about returning to the party. She

needed to say her piece to Jeb, soon. But a part of her—
what Jeb would call the one hundred percent pure
chicken part—hesitated.

"Cluck, cluck," she muttered as she stepped out of
the motor home and began walking back to the party.

CHAPTER NINE

JEB DRAINED HIS BEER and set the bottle back on the bar, his reply to Dixon's question about the third pit stop distracted. Shouldn't Cara be back by now? He'd seen her rounding up the boys with her usual blend of tenderness and firmness, then Dylan and Shane had run over to tell him good-night.

Now, he was anxious to lay eyes on her in that dress again. Cara had been gussied up for dates before, but he'd never seen her look so gorgeous. It was eating him up that she'd worn that creation for Ryder…but it didn't stop him wanting her. He was beginning to wonder if anything could.

Everything about her was beautiful. Not just her face and figure in that incredible dress, but her way with the kids, her natural ease with everyone, from the sponsors to the waiters.

"You listening to a word I say, Jeb?" Dixon asked mildly.

"Sorry." He shook his head, clearing it.

"You can be excused a little distraction after a win," Dixon said.

"It's warm in here," he said. "Too many people." About fifty too many. "Excuse me while I step outside, Dixon."

Downstairs, he breathed in the California air, scented with cooling pavement and a lingering smell of rubber, and felt better. He strolled along the row of suites that fronted onto the pit road.

He'd been walking a couple of minutes when he heard the tap of heels coming toward him. Then Cara rounded the corner past the infield care center.

She saw him from a few yards away, and her face lit up. Jeb's chest tightened.

"Boys okay?" he asked as she reached him.

"Exhausted, but very happy." She wrapped her fingers around the chain-link fence that enclosed the parking lot for suite guests. "I was coming to find you."

Now, that he hadn't expected.

"Could we take a walk?" she asked. "Just for a few minutes?"

"Of course." Jeb started off at a brisk pace, wanting to put as much distance between her and her date as he could.

She laughed behind him, and the sound skittered over him in the night air. "If you're going to go this fast, I'd better fetch my sneakers."

Jeb slowed down, let her catch him up.

They passed the care center and headed into the open area that earlier had held hospitality tents. As they sidestepped a trash can, she moved closer to him and his hand brushed hers, setting off a chain reaction from his head to his toes.

He might as well admit he was no closer to putting her out of his mind than when he first resolved to.

After a long moment, Cara renewed the gap between

them. "Lucy spent her evening drawing a picture of you winning today's race," she said.

"She's a cutie." From there they moved into a conversation about the kids, then the race. He'd always loved Cara's dissection of a race—she tended to focus on things other people didn't see, like the reactions atop the war wagons.

They reached the edge of the motor home lot and turned back.

"Are you interested in my crew chief?" Jeb asked.

Cara stumbled, and he took her arm. Her skin was warm and satiny.

"No," she said.

"Good." Then, when she looked up at him, "He dates a lot of women. I wouldn't want you to get hurt."

"You date a lot of women, too. Or you always did."

"I've grown out of that." He released her arm, but caught her fingers in his. *Friends hold hands...sometimes.*

Jeb found it hard to concentrate on putting one foot in front of another as they walked in silence for another minute. Then she said, "I already told Ryder I'm not interested. He was fine about it."

He stopped. "I'm pleased to hear that."

Silence fell.

"You know that list I gave you?" she said.

He reached into his pocket. "This one?"

She eyed it as if it was a bomb. "You brought it to the party?"

"I was reading it before I came out."

"Oh." She swallowed. "There's another name. One more to add."

"I didn't bring a pen."

She drew an audible breath. "It's me."

The list fluttered from Jeb's fingers to the ground.

"Don't say anything," she ordered quickly. "This might sound completely out of left field, but those qualities that you're looking for… You know, liking NASCAR, liking you for yourself, not your status."

"Chemistry," he added.

She nodded. "I believe I meet those criteria. Most of them."

Jeb picked a fine time to turn stupid. He couldn't quite believe it, but it sounded as if she was saying—

"How about it?" she asked. "Will you put me on the list?" She closed her eyes, bit her lip.

"Cara, honey, as of right now, you *are* the list." Jeb hauled her into his arms.

Her eyes flew open. She put a hand to his chest, and the heat seared him. "You don't have to decide right away," she said nervously.

Uh-oh, another minute and she'd be backing out, convincing herself there was some reason they couldn't do this.

"Too late, honey. Stop talking." He grinned down at her…then lowered his mouth to hers.

FIRE. THAT WAS THE ONLY WORD to describe the extreme heat that swept Cara the moment Jeb's lips met hers. For an instant, it reminded her of that first kiss, the one she'd never entirely forgotten…but this was different. This one packed a power that sucked up all the oxygen and filled her with heady longing.

His hands moved to her waist, drawing her closer.

It wasn't possible to be close enough. Cara opened her mouth to him, and almost sobbed with relief as he claimed her, explored her, tasted her.

He pushed her back against the wall of the care center, and she wound her arms around his neck, buried her hands in his dark hair. She pressed her curves against him, reveling in his need for her.

Jeb groaned as he pulled away. "If we don't stop now, I'm going to make love to you right here."

Make love with Jeb? Cara's body shrieked *yes*. Her brain had a different take. Her hands skimmed his shoulders. "Jeb…"

He sighed. "I know. Not now. For once I agree with your absurd rules."

"I need time to get my head around this."

"You don't get to chicken out," he warned.

"After that kiss? Are you kidding?" She pressed her lips to the side of his neck. "But you know me. I don't rush things."

"Yeah." His finger trailed down her cheek.

"I'm tired. Will you pass on my excuses to Dixon and Ryder?"

"Sure," he said, "so long as you and the kids fly back to Charlotte with me tomorrow."

"On your plane?"

He grinned. "You bet." Then he took her hands, ran his thumbs over her palms. "You have nine hours to get your head around this, honey. Tomorrow, this thing is official."

Her entire body thrilled to the promise beneath the words. "You don't think it's too sudden?"

"I think sixteen years getting to know each other is just about enough."

"There is that," she agreed.

His hand curled around hers. "I'll walk you back to the motor home."

"No need. There are security guards everywhere, and I'd like some time to cool off before I face the sitter."

He agreed with evident reluctance. Then planted a hard kiss on her lips that ensured she wouldn't think of anyone but him.

CARA MIGHT HAVE HAD a sleepless night, but she hadn't wasted those hours spent staring at the crack of light between the edge of the blind and the window in Ryder's motor home.

First she'd allowed herself an enjoyably frustrating reliving of that kiss. Then, it was time to figure out what would happen next.

She could scarcely believe Jeb wanted her as much as she wanted him, when he could have anyone. Yet on one level it made sense. If they could make it work, she and Jeb would be the great friends they'd always been…with some hot sex thrown in.

Scorching.

She shoved the sheets aside and let the cool air waft over her body.

"Mama?" Lucy called from the fold-down bunk bed in the tiny hallway.

Cara twitched the blind aside and peered at her watch in the glow of the security light outside. 6:00 a.m. Jeb had said they'd have to leave by seven, so she might as well get up. "Coming, sweetie."

By the time they reached the L.A. Ontario airport a

few miles from the track, Cara was as nervous as a sixteen-year-old on her first date. What if she'd got it wrong? What if Jeb hadn't wanted more than one kiss? What if—?

"Mrs. Rivers?" A young man in a pilot's uniform—surely he was too young to be a pilot?—greeted her. "Jeb's already onboard, he asked me to escort you and your family to the plane."

"Thanks." Cara mustered a smile for the pilot-boy. Darn it, a minute ago she'd felt sixteen, and now she felt sixty. Why would Jeb want someone like her, who had no abs to speak of and who liked to be in bed with the light out by ten?

Then they were walking up the steps of the plane and it was too late to insist she'd make her own way home.

The co-pilot greeted them in the doorway. Behind him was Jeb.

"Hey, kids, welcome to my new plane." He'd bought the aircraft last year. "Why don't you go explore?"

The children needed no further invitation. As Cara made a point of examining every aspect of the plane's décor, rather than meeting Jeb's eyes, she heard Dylan exclaiming. Over the TV set. Good grief, hadn't she raised her kids to do more than watch TV?

"Cara." Jeb's deep voice came from right behind her, startling her.

"Mmm?" She fingered the silk fabric wall paneling. "This is beautiful."

Strong hands grasped her shoulders, turned her to face him.

"Cara," he said again, and in that one word she knew he hadn't changed his mind, and that he wanted her. He cupped her face in his hands and kissed her thoroughly…but briefly, releasing her at around the same moment as the kids exhausted the potential of the TV remote control.

"Wow," he said. "I need to do that again."

Me, too. "The kids are exhausted. I'm sure they'll fall asleep when we're up in the air." At his feet she saw an open locker, full of games and movies. "You might need to pretend you don't have any onboard entertainment."

"Uncle Jeb, do you have any movies?" Shane called.

"Sorry, kids," Jeb said without a flicker of shame, as he kicked the locker closed. "I'm afraid this flight will be pretty boring."

IT TOOK NEARLY AN HOUR for Dylan, the last of the kids, to drop off, but at last they had privacy. Cara and Jeb were sitting next to each other on the couch, and he'd made sure to keep close, relishing the warmth of her leg against his. But proximity had made the longing even harder to bear. As soon as Dylan's eyes had been closed for half a minute, he drew Cara into his arms.

"I thought he'd never go to sleep," he murmured.

"Me, too." Heartfelt relief in her tone—how he loved to hear that.

He'd been awake most of the night, convinced she wouldn't turn up for this morning's flight. Even now she was here, he felt he had to hold on to her. This whole thing felt…too easy.

As if he'd decided he wanted a woman to share his life with, and five minutes later, here was Cara, and her kids, everything he'd dreamed of. She was the one who'd warned him it didn't happen that way.

Nothing came easy in NASCAR, either. If this had been a race, about now he'd find Garrett Clark had sneaked up behind him and stolen a pass before Jeb even knew the guy was there.

"Jeb, are you okay?"

Her blue eyes were focused on him, bright with interest. Jeb tried to shake off this odd case of nerves. Cara was here, she wanted him, what else mattered?

"Where were we?" he mused.

"Right about here?" With unexpected boldness, Cara kissed him. Oh, yeah, it didn't get much better than this. Not without a bed. Jeb tugged her into his lap, and deepened the kiss.

They kept a wary eye on the kids, but it was amazing how much seriously good making out you could manage if you kept quiet.

Cara was soft and supple beneath his hands, perfectly shaped for him. She smelled of jasmine, and those little noises she made…practically purring with delight. He should have known she was so tactile, she was always hugging the kids, but to have this attention lavished on him…once again, he gave himself up to the moment.

When the cockpit door handle rattled, they jerked apart. Adam, the pilot, discreetly took his time about getting the door open. When he entered the cabin, they were sitting side by side, and all Cara's buttons were in the right place.

"We'll be landing in about an hour," Adam said. "Do you want me to heat up some food for you?"

"We can get it," Jeb said. He knew the co-pilot was capable of handling things in the cockpit, but he much preferred to have the pilot actually flying the plane.

When they were alone, he drank in the sight of Cara's face, her eyes bright, her lips blurred by his kisses. "We'd better talk," he said. "That's why I invited you on this flight."

"Is that the reason?" she asked, all mischievous innocence.

"*One* of the reasons." He kissed her nose.

"You're right, we need to discuss the kids, among other things. I'm happy for them to know we're together—I think they'll be thrilled."

"Good." He celebrated that piece of news with another kiss, ignoring another niggle of *too easy*. He didn't think he'd ever get enough of this woman. Was it too soon to propose?

"It's early days," he said, "but you know I'm not messing you around, and with the kids involved we need to be clear about where we're headed."

"Absolutely," she agreed. "I hardly got any sleep last night, thinking all this through."

He hoped to be keeping her awake for a better reason very soon. "So where did your thinking get you?"

She eased away from him so she could meet his eyes. "I guess the number one challenge will be making time for each other."

He frowned as he got up to fetch a couple of sodas from the bar fridge. "We'll be spending a lot more time together." Much of that in bed, if he had his way. He handed her a cola.

"*Some* more," she agreed. "The kids and I can probably make it to every third race—we'll figure out something that doesn't disrupt my shifts at the hospital or their schooling."

He felt winded, as if he'd just been knocked into the corner by a car he hadn't seen coming. "What?"

She grimaced. "It's not ideal, you and I won't get as much time together as we might like…but it'll be more than we have now." She pulled the tab on her soda can.

It felt as if they were in two different conversations. Two different grooves. "You do know that I want to get married?" he said. "That if this works out, you'll be my wife?"

"Jeb, I want to get married, too." She patted his hand. The way he'd seen her pat the kids over some childish anxiety.

"So if we get married, what exactly are you suggesting will change, other than having my ring on your finger?" he asked.

"In terms of our daily routines, not a lot," she said patiently, "though I'll be attending more races. But we'll be…intimate. A couple. You'll be a father to the kids."

Her calm logic was producing a correspondingly *illogical* response in Jeb.

"The way I hear it," he said, "you plan to go on living your life just as you have been, only now you're parceling out a few crumbs of your time to me."

She stared. "That's not true."

"Then why don't you explain—" his voice had risen, so Jeb took a calming breath before he continued more quietly "—exactly what you've decided our relationship should be."

She didn't appear to hear the irony. "It would be what we both want," she said. "Marriage, family."

Her words came back to him. *There's marriage, and there's marriage.*

"I know what kind of marriage you had with Pat," he said. "That's what I want."

Consternation filled her eyes. "Jeb, you…you're very dear to me."

Who would believe such lukewarm sentiment could hit so hard?

"You make me sound like your grandmother's best china," he growled.

"But I'm not going through that again." She eased back in her seat. "You know how cut up I was when Pat died. How brokenhearted the kids were. No way do I want my life to be so tightly bound up in someone else's that if they left or…or died, I'd fall apart."

"You didn't fall apart when Pat—"

"I won't go through that again," she snapped.

"What exactly are you saying? You want to marry me, but you don't love me?"

She tensed. "Of course I love you, you're my dearest friend. But, Jeb, I can't love you the way I loved Pat." She chafed her arms. "That two-melded-into-one kind of way. When you love someone that deeply…when something goes wrong, it hurts."

"So you and I would have some kind of second-rate, watered-down marriage?" he said slowly.

CHAPTER TEN

"No," Cara protested, all the anxieties she'd ever had about a guy like Jeb suddenly flooding back. He was unpredictable, volatile, demanding. "We'd be happy. Jeb, you're muddying things. You can't tell me you're wildly in love with me."

"Why should I love you, if you won't love me?" he demanded.

She felt a shaft of pain behind her ribs. "Spoken like a man who has no idea how love works."

"You can argue the semantics," he said. "But when I get married, it'll be the most important thing in my life. I won't settle for anything less than my wife's full commitment, from day one."

They glared at each other, anger and resentment simmering.

"Jeb…" Cara set her untouched soda down on the table in front of her and spread her hands, striving for reasonableness. Then she stopped. The intensity of the passion between them had left her off-balance. As if she was free-falling, rather than safely ensconced aboard his private jet.

"I know exactly what you're doing," he said. "The same as you did sixteen years ago. Chickening out of something that doesn't fit the neat parameters you've set for your life."

"We were kids back then…."

"And one of us grew up." He stood, and moved out of the cozy seating arrangement they'd shared. "Cara, I don't want what you're offering."

"I'm offering you *me*," she whispered.

"You're offering me a *part* of you."

She couldn't deny it. She'd spent nearly four years erecting the barricades that would save her from future heartbreak. And now Jeb expected her to tear them down and let him into her deepest places?

"Please, try to understand." She fumbled to undo her seat belt, and stood to join him. "It's bad enough knowing something could happen to one of the kids at any time and take them away from me. It's terrifying. I don't want my relationship with you, or with any man, to feel like that."

"So if I dropped dead tomorrow, you wouldn't care?"

Something stabbed deep. "Of course I would. But it wouldn't be like losing Pat."

He flinched, and she knew she'd hurt him. Too bad. She didn't feel like that about Jeb, and she didn't intend to.

He shoved his hands in his pockets. "I don't know much about love, but I know a hell of a lot about racing," he said. "I know you don't win without putting everything into it. I'm not prepared to do less, or to accept less. If second place isn't good enough for me out on the track, it's sure as hell not good enough for my family."

She licked her lips. "What are you saying?"

"I'm saying you have to choose. All or nothing."

Cara tried to imagine never kissing him again, and already it hurt. "Jeb, please, don't."

"All or nothing," he repeated.

Dammit, she'd always known he was dangerous; she could feel splinters piercing her heart. "You expect me to trust you one minute, and the next you're dumping me? I knew this would happen."

His head jerked back. "This is *your* decision."

"My decision is to be with you, to love you as best I can. You're saying that's not good enough." How could she have been so stupid as to believe he was no longer a risk to her?

He folded his arms, and didn't speak.

Oh, yes, he was dumping her, all right. And it hurt. Thank goodness she hadn't allowed her feelings for him to deepen the way he claimed to want.

It was bad enough as it was. She would be just one of many women he'd kissed and moved on from. Whereas he would be the only man she could remember kissing, beside her husband.

Which he'd always been, but now that memory would be knife-sharp.

IF JEB'S LIFE was a race, Cara's announcement that she didn't plan to love him as much as she'd loved Pat was the equivalent of that crash at Daytona.

It overturned him.

It was too late to put his passion for her back in the box and go after some other woman. Now that he'd held Cara in his arms, now that he knew her kisses were even more seductive than they'd been when they were teens…he couldn't let go.

But he couldn't settle for the kind of life she wanted.

What made her think she could make up the rules for their relationship? he fumed, as he climbed into his car for qualifying at Las Vegas the weekend after California. It was typical, infuriating Cara behavior.

Fueled by frustration, he qualified tenth. On Sunday, he worked his way up to a sixth-place finish. Ryder was thrilled, the sponsor was happy. The only person who was miserable was Jeb.

He missed Cara. So much, he wondered as he grabbed his bag from his motor home if he should call her, invite her and the kids over for a meal.

Or maybe he should drop in at her place.

But suddenly he was sick of seeing her on Pat's turf, and he didn't want to sit on a couch where she might have been making out with some soccer coach.

Besides, he was smart enough to know where he might end up if he crawled back to her. Taking whatever measly part of her life she offered.

Thankfully, he was able to resist, which he put down to his ability as a race car driver to see the big picture, as well as the moment.

He caught a ride to the airport with Ben and Susie Edmonds, a couple he respected hugely. Ben had finished near the back of the field, a common occurrence for him recently, so he wasn't happy. But Susie knew just how to handle her husband, and her loving attention drew Ben out of his funk. They were clearly crazy about each other, after years of marriage, though Jeb didn't doubt they'd faced their challenges.

Cara could take a lesson from them, he thought grimly.

He sat up straighter. If Cara didn't trust him on the subject of their relationship, maybe she would trust someone like Susie. Both women were members of the Tuesday Tarts, that mysterious female get-together the men didn't inquire too closely into, for fear they might not like what they heard. But he'd bet money those women talked about their love lives.

Ben cuffed his shoulder. "Penny for your thoughts. They look a whole lot more exciting than mine."

"Susie," Jeb said. "I need your help."

BY THE TUESDAY after Las Vegas, Cara felt as if her emotions had been sliced, diced and shredded. She hadn't even watched the race on TV, since she was on a Jeb-free diet, but that hadn't stopped her wallowing.

Nor had it made her any less mad at Jeb. How dare he demand so much of her, when he knew what she'd lost?

Too raw after their bust-up, she'd skipped the Tuesday Tarts gathering she'd promised Sheila Trueblood she would attend last week. She hadn't planned to go tonight, either.

Then Grace Clark called.

"You have to come to Tarts tonight," Grace said.

"I'm not really—"

"I need to talk to you, it's important."

"Is it about Lucy?" Cara wondered if her daughter had done something to upset Grace's Bella during the playdate they'd had after California. Or vice versa.

"Indirectly it is," Grace said. "Just say you'll be there."

If it was about one of her kids, Cara didn't have a choice.

"I'll be there."

BY THE TIME SHE REACHED Maudie's, Cara was more than ready for the glass of red wine she knew Sheila would have waiting. She said a quick hello to Mellie Donovan, the waitress who'd been working at the diner for a couple of weeks.

"Sheila and I are taking turns minding the store. They're waiting for you back there." She waved Cara behind the counter.

"Cara!" The chorus of warm greetings as she walked into the room in the back that served as the Tarts' meeting place heartened her. Adjacent to the oversize pantry and storage area, the space was a staff break room by day. Tonight, the chef's table, covered with a crisp white cloth, held two desserts—including the famous lemon meringue pie, if Cara wasn't mistaken—coffee and, more importantly, wine.

She made a circuit, hugging Sheila, Patsy Grosso, Grace Clark, Susie Edmonds and Rue Larrabee, owner of the Cut'N'Chat salon and founder of the Tarts. Then she shook hands with a woman she hadn't met, but who was apparently now a Tarts regular: Emma-Lee Dalton, personal assistant to the owner of Double S Racing.

One of the women on the list she'd given Jeb.

How could she have been so stupid? Emma-Lee was gorgeous!

"It's nice to meet you," Cara lied, before she settled next to Grace, glass in hand, on the maroon velvet-upholstered couch—one of Sheila's thrift-store bargains.

"It's so good to see you all," she said to the wider assembly.

"Hold that thought," Patsy said.

Something in her tone alerted Cara. "What's going on?"

Patsy grinned. "Didn't anyone tell you? We're staging an intervention?"

"Who's the victim?" Cara was halfway through the question when she realized all eyes on were on her. *Uh-oh.*

"Did Jeb talk to you?" she demanded, scanning the room for guilty faces. Because a part of her had been surprised that Jeb had given up so easily when she'd told him it was over.

Grace nodded. Then Patsy. Then Sheila lifted her whiskey glass in a toast. One by one, every woman in the room confessed she'd gone over to the dark side. Except Emma-Lee, and Cara wasn't much disposed to like her, anyway.

Torn between an irrational pleasure that Jeb was still pursuing her and mortification that he'd shared their private business, Cara tightened her fingers around the stem of her wineglass. "You told me this was about Lucy," she accused Grace.

"Your relationship with Jeb affects all of your children," Grace said, in her earth-mother style.

"Jeb and I don't have a relationship."

"I remember the first time I met you," Patsy said. "It was before you even met Pat. Jeb introduced us—he was smitten."

"Jeb's easily smitten," Cara said. She didn't actually remember that first encounter with Patsy.

"Maybe back then," Patsy agreed. "He was one of the hard-partiers. That was the main difference between him and Pat. But these days he's a little more measured in his approach."

"Since Pat died it's occurred to just about everyone that you two should get together," Rue chimed in.

Cara prayed she wasn't blushing, but there was enough interest in the women's faces to suggest she was. "Jeb and I are old friends."

"That's a great place to start, honey," Susie Edmonds said. "You have a lot of common ground."

Honey reminded Cara of Jeb, and she felt a loneliness at her core, the kind that had hit her when Pat died. Back then, Jeb had eased the loneliness.

"If common ground is so important, why did you set Jeb up with your cousin who hates motorsports?" she asked acerbically.

"Oops, my bad." Susie smirked, unrepentant.

"Cara, you've been dating again, so why not Jeb?" Sheila wasn't about to allow the distraction. "He adores your kids, you should hear him going on about Dylan's engine instincts and Shane's lethal right boot. Not to mention Lucy's artworks."

Cara hardened her heart. "We want different things, it would never work."

"Haven't we all been there?" Grace said, one eyebrow arched. She looked and sounded so like Patsy, every woman in the room swiveled her head between the two. If there was ever proof that genes would prevail, Grace was it.

Tears sprang to Patsy's eyes. She still hadn't gotten used to the idea that her long-lost daughter was back.

"It's okay, Mom." Grace was experimenting with the word, and it came out hesitant, breathy and tender. She squeezed Patsy's hand.

"Ignore me." But Patsy squeezed back, hard. "Cara, Jeb says you don't want to fall in love with him."

"I can't believe he told you that!" She would kill him. Except she wasn't ever going near him again. "Besides, he's not in love with me."

"He's gone to some lengths to get your attention, for a guy who's not in love," Grace observed.

Cara took a slug of her wine. "He's got some idea about settling down. I'm the nearest, easiest option."

"Ah, yes, that's how love works," Patsy said sagely. "Not."

"He's just determined to have things his way," Cara said. "You know what he's like."

To her shock, every woman in the room started laughing.

"Unlike you, who never pushes for what she wants?" Susie suggested.

"I have three kids, it's my job to fight for what's best for them. You understand," she appealed to Grace. "You lost a husband, you know how hard it is to start over."

Grace sipped her cabernet. "Todd will always be part of my life. Getting over his death was hard. But I wouldn't be on my own just because I was too scared to take a risk."

Which made Cara sound like a wimp.

"Besides, once I fell in love with Garrett, chickening out wasn't an option." Everyone laughed at the cat-got-the-cream satisfaction in Grace's tone.

"That's the difference," Cara said, relieved. "I'm not

in love with Jeb." Not everyone was like Grace, who was clearly an amazing woman. Cara was more... ordinary. She wasn't looking for an extraordinary passion.

"I tell you, Cara, if you have a shot at happiness with Jeb, don't throw it away without trying to find a compromise," Susie said. "You don't get offered a chance at love every day, and you never know what's around the corner."

"That's exactly the point," Cara said. "I don't want to invite someone else into my life that I might lose."

"NASCAR is incredibly safe these days," Susie began.

"It's not about racing, it's about the million and one things that could go wrong at any moment."

The other women looked baffled. Jeb had obviously done a great job of getting them on his side.

"You don't need to worry about Jeb," Cara said. "He'll find someone else by next week." Probably Emma-Lee.

"I wouldn't bet on it," Emma-Lee said, unaware she was on Jeb's list. "I keep an eye on these things, and I tell you, lately Jeb's been, like, a monk."

Laughter rippled around the room at the unlikely image.

Cara took advantage of the lifting of tension. "I appreciate your concern and your loyalty more than you could know. But please can we talk about something else?"

She glanced around, zoomed in. "Like Sheila. Has anyone asked her why Gil Sizemore hangs around here so much?"

All eyes turned to Maudie's hapless owner. Cara considered making a run for the door, then decided to stick around and enjoy seeing someone else squirm.

JEB CALLED CARA early on Wednesday, as she was rushing to get ready for work.

"How was last night?" he asked, without preamble.

"It was an ambush, and I didn't appreciate it." She tucked the phone between chin and shoulder as she pulled her hair into its ponytail. "You know what I'm willing to offer, Jeb, and that hasn't changed."

"You mean, you're still a coward."

Ouch! "You won't be wanting to marry one of those, then," she said snottily.

He chuckled into the phone.

She was miserable, and he thought this was funny?

"I have a Plan B," he said. "You need to come to Atlanta this weekend."

"There's no point." She sat on the bed and pushed first her right foot into a sneaker, then her left.

"Would you agree you are a totally unreasonable woman who refuses to consider anyone else's perspective?"

"No, I would not," she said sharply.

"Prove it," he said. "Come to Atlanta with an open mind. Spend the weekend with me, officially this time, and consider the possibility of falling in love with me. Crazy in love."

She shivered. "Why would I do that?"

"Because I'll undertake to consider with an open mind whether I can live with what you're offering," he said. "You and the kids can have my motor home, and

I'll get Ryder to return the favor he owes me. We'll have a weekend together as a family, and see what falls out the other end."

"What's the catch?" she asked.

"No catch. One last-ditch effort, then if we haven't found something we agree on, we call it quits. Amicably."

Amicably. She sure didn't want to go on the way they were, with this hurt and hostility.

"You're just hoping I'll fall for you," she said.

"You bet." A smile beneath the words. "Hey, all's fair in love, war and racing."

"Well, I won't."

"You're hoping I'll lower my expectations," he said. "And I can assure you I won't. But one thing I've learned from racing, sometimes the darnedest things happen."

She checked her appearance in the mirror over her dressing table. She was getting frown lines. "Don't underestimate me," she said. "I won't change my mind."

"All the more reason for you to come to Atlanta. What's the worst that could happen?" he cajoled. "That you and I get to make out, and the kids have a great time watching the race?"

There had to be something worse, she just couldn't figure out what it was. She was too preoccupied with the thought of making out.

"So, you want to fly down, or drive?" He had a nerve, presuming she would agree.

"Drive," she said. "By the time we go through all the airport hassle, we might as well take the car."

"I'll pick you up Thursday lunchtime."

She was about to tell him there was no way they'd all fit into his sports car so they'd have to take her SUV, but he hung up. Probably so she couldn't change her mind.

Cara stared at the phone. So, Jeb hoped to convince her to do things his way. Two could play at that game.

What if she got him so hooked on her and the kids that he'd accept what he considered her substandard offer of a relationship based on friendship and sex?

It seemed an underhanded method of getting what she wanted. But as Jeb himself said, all was fair in love, war and racing.

She scrolled through the numbers stored in the phone, then made a call to Rue at the Cut'N'Chat.

CHAPTER ELEVEN

"WHAT IS *THAT?*" CARA pointed at the bright red SUV in her driveway.

"My new car," Jeb said, enjoying her shock.

"You sold your sports car?"

"Of course not." He relieved her of the bag she was carrying. "I've added a family vehicle to my portfolio. Climb aboard, kids."

The children ran to obey, drawn to the shiny new vehicle. Who wasn't father material now?

"You low-down snake," she said.

Which he took to mean she was impressed by his tactics. "Thanks," he said. "New haircut?"

He wasn't the only one fighting to win. Cara's hair had been cut in a feathery, layered style that made her look younger, more carefree. She wore figure-hugging jeans and a semisheer pale pink blouse he hadn't seen before. With the top two buttons undone.

She caught him looking and put her hands on her hips, which threw her curves into prominence. If this was fighting dirty, Jeb was all in favor.

He was strong, even stronger than she, and no matter how gorgeous, how sexy, she was, he wasn't about to back down on his demand for her whole heart.

Because when she'd walked away from his airplane without looking back, the truth had socked him on the jaw.

He loved her. Really loved her, in the way that would freak her out. He didn't know where he'd come up with the idea that love was something that would grow in line with the relationship. His love for Cara had sprung into exuberant life and refused to heed any suggestion to slow down.

It was everything she'd said love should be, and more. Joyous, uncomfortable, hope-filled, painful, tender…and sharp and wounding as a rusty nail.

Now that Jeb had been afflicted, the only way to live with it was to convince Cara to love him back.

When he got her and the kids to Atlanta, he planned to sweep them all off their feet. And into his arms.

THE KIDS READ or dozed all the way to Atlanta, where they settled into the motor home, and Sally, Jeb's driver, barbecued dinner for them. Cara had worked the night shift last night and had very little sleep, so she and the kids went to bed early. Jeb did manage to sneak in a good-night kiss.

On Friday, he qualified on the pole for Sunday's race, a cause for major celebration—including a lingering kiss from Cara. He took her and the kids out for dinner to a local pizza place, kids' choice. And proceeded to play footsie with her.

When she seemed to like that, he held her hand across the table. And when they got back to the motor home and put on a DVD for the kids to watch, he and Cara took the "back row" and managed some discreet but hot kisses during the animated movie's more gripping moments.

So far, neither of them was backing down in their game of relationship chicken, though they hadn't actually talked about the future.

But Jeb was confident Cara was softening up. He could see it in her eyes, hear it in the warmth in her voice, sense it in her pliant response to his kisses.

Yep, this couldn't be headed in a better direction if it was GPS guided.

THE RACE STARTED in the same charmed way everything else had gone that weekend.

The moment the green flag dropped, Jeb surged ahead of Eli Ward, who'd started alongside him on the front row. For five laps, he held that position. Ward got ahead on lap six, but two laps later, Jeb was out in front. They ran like that, trading the lead with the occasional incursion from one of the farther back drivers, until the first pit stop. Jeb's car was overheating, but Ryder and the team had the front grille cleared of debris and the car back on track in a creditable 13.1 seconds.

There were more contenders for the lead after that, but Jeb stayed in the top five, confident he could find his way to the front again when he had to. The car was great. Once, Cara borrowed Ryder's headset and told him in a sultry voice to get a hurry on because she missed him there in the pits.

What better incentive could a guy have to finish a race as fast as humanly possible?

They were one lap short of halfway when Bart

Branch nudged him, knocking the No. 464 car sideways at the precise moment that Zack Matheson was passing him.

The crunch of metal on metal came on both sides. Being the filling in a stock car sandwich was never a good thing. Something had to give, and Jeb felt an obstruction against his right front tire.

He still had control of the car, but it wasn't going anywhere faster than a snail's pace.

Ryder came over the headset. "From what I can see, you have too much body damage to carry on."

Jeb cursed. "I'll bring her in so you can take a look."

Carefully, he made his way to the bottom of the track. He was almost there when Rafael O'Bryan failed to avoid him. He shunted into Jeb. Hard.

CARA HAD BEEN in the pits through the first couple of pit stops, but then she returned to the motor home lot, where Patsy Grosso had invited her and a bunch of the other women to watch the race on the huge TV that was one of Dean's pleasures—the largest TV in the motor home lot, Patsy claimed with a resigned sigh.

The kids were all in Grace's motor home next door, where they had two TVs going—one with the race, one with an animated film.

"Jeb's on form today," Grace commented.

"So is Garrett," Cara said, mainly to be polite. Jeb looked way stronger than Garrett.

He'd sounded relaxed and confident, when she spoke to him over his headset.

Confident in more than the race. Because against her will, this weekend was bringing her around to his way of thinking. His new car, all the things he'd done that showed how important she and the kids were to him…how could any woman not melt in response?

Jeb had obviously figured that out.

She wondered what would happen tonight. They would return to Charlotte right after the race—she'd offered to drive, since Jeb would be tired—and she was hoping he would come inside when they reached her place. Then, after the kids were in bed…

"Bad boy, Bart," Susie Edmonds said, as Bart Branch clipped Jeb's car.

Cara watched the No. 464 car. Her gaze sharpened. Jeb was about to hit Zack Matheson.

When the crunch came, her heart felt as if it was being squeezed in a vise. Somehow he made it out of the sandwich and headed for the bottom of the track. But before he could reach safety, Rafael O'Bryan plowed into him, shunting Jeb's car into a spin.

A sob burst from her.

"Cara, you okay?" Patsy muted the sound.

She didn't speak, her eyes were glued to the screen. As she waited for Jeb's car to stop, her heart felt as if it had been ripped from her chest.

She'd never been so terrified in her life.

Safety crews ran toward the car. She had to move. Panic forced her to her feet, propelled her toward the door.

"Where are you going?" Grace turned to the other women. "She's crying."

Was she? She had no idea.

"Cara…" Patsy began.

Cara didn't hear the rest. Once out of the motor

home lot, she began shoving her way through the crowd of fans. She had to get to the infield care center, which would be Jeb's first port of call…unless he was so badly hurt that he… *No.*

Her breath came in heaving sobs, her lungs screamed for air, but all she could think about was Jeb. Hurt, dying, leaving her.

How dare he?

She'd seen him crash dozens of times, and never done more than wince and hold her breath until he was out of the car. It had never occurred to her he might be hurt.

Please, she prayed. *Please.*

She reached the care center just as Jeb walked out. A corner of her mind registered the way his face lit up as he saw her. "Cara, honey."

It was the last straw. She flew at him, ignored the arms he opened and whacked him with her purse. Hard.

"Ouch." Jeb took a step backward.

"You jerk." Smack, she hit him again. "You rotten, sneaky…" A blow from her purse punctuated each adjective.

Jeb grabbed her by the shoulders. "Stop that. Are you crazy?"

Now she could feel the tears on her face, dripping into her mouth. "I'm not doing anything. Ever. With you. Again. Never." The words came out as hiccupping, ranting sobs.

"Cara, for goodness' sake." Jeb glanced around. "Do you want to be on TV in hysterics? Do you want the kids to see this?"

It was enough to make her draw breath. Jeb took advantage of her momentary self-control to grab her hand and drag her away from the converging reporters.

"I'm not going with you," she snapped.

"You damn well are." He quickened his pace, forcing her to jog to keep up.

When they reached his team's hauler, he pushed her up the steps and into the dim interior.

"What was that about?" he demanded. "No, don't tell me yet." He tugged her through the hauler to the office at the front. In there, he pushed her down onto the built-in couch, then closed the door firmly.

"Well?" he demanded.

He looked as if he thought she was insane. If she wasn't, she soon would be.

"You crashed," she accused him.

"Ah." He shifted, folded his arms across his chest. "That wasn't a crash, just Bart Branch being an idiot and O'Bryan too slow on the brakes."

"You could have been hurt."

"I'm fine. I wouldn't even have gone to the care center if some official hadn't made me. The doc gave me the all clear right away."

She buried her face in her hands, shock setting in. "I don't ever want to go through this again," she sobbed.

Jeb scratched his head. "The crash I had at Daytona was far worse, so bad I thought I was up for some serious injury, and you laughed." His voice softened. "Cara, I don't understand you."

"We can't date," she said. "It's over. I'm not going to sit here week after week in terror."

His jaw set. "Cara, you saw Pat crash almost as

many times as I did. You used to get upset, but nothing like this."

"That's because back then I didn't know what it would feel like to lose someone I love," she said. "I can't go through that again, Jeb. I can't."

He seemed to be trembling. She pulled herself together, despite the new surge of panic, and she half rose from the seat. "What's wrong, do you feel faint? I'll get an ambulance."

His laugh startled her. "Cara, honey, you just said you love me."

"I didn't." Then she realized. *I did. I do. I love Jeb.*

Even as her brain protested, her heart swelled with love for the man who'd been a father to her children, her best friend in the world and the best damn kisser she knew. Who made the world a more exciting place, and made her more alive in it. She moaned.

"Hey, it's not all bad." He pulled her to him, stroked her hair. She felt the press of his lips above her temple. "If it's any consolation, I love you, too."

He was shaking again…only this time it was with laughter. Cara thumped his chest.

"Honey, I know physical violence isn't how you show love to the kids, so maybe you could tone it down a little with me?" He was laughing outright now.

"You…you smug, smart-aleck NASCAR driver," she accused. "You think because I love you I'll put up with this? I won't. I might have been stupid enough to fall in love, but I'm smart enough to get myself out of it."

"Then you'd be smarter than I am," he said. "I adore you, Cara, in a way I never thought possible, and it's not going away."

Fresh tears pricked her eyes. "I gave you a weekend, like I promised, and I've made my decision. I don't want this, Jeb. I don't want you."

He released her, and she felt cold. "Don't do this."

She shivered. "I have to."

His face hardened. "Is this your idea of giving us a shot? One tiny setback, not even a real one, and you bail? What kind of example is that for your kids?"

"My kids lost their father," she ground out. "They don't need to go through that again, either."

"And they coped with that loss because they have a strong, smart mother showing them the way," he said. "That's not what I'm seeing now."

"Maybe I'm not as strong or as smart as you think," Cara retorted.

He made to take her in his arms again, and she jumped backward. She couldn't risk hanging around, having him persuade her against her better judgment. "I'm looking out for myself and my children," she said. "That's all."

The contempt on his face almost made her cry.

As she stalked out of the hauler, she faced the truth. She'd lost everything.

Lost the precious sense of security she'd been building since Pat died. Lost faith in her own ability to cope. Lost her heart to Jeb.

CHAPTER TWELVE

TUESDAY WAS THE FOURTH ANNIVERSARY of Pat's death. Only her husband would have gone jet-boating during a lingering winter on the grounds it was officially spring, Cara thought fondly, as she drove to the cemetery just before seven in the morning. A bunch of flowers—white lilies and red snapdragons, Pat's team colors—lay on the passenger seat next to her.

Pat had been the most sensible of men in everything other than racing.

Usually, she made this trip with Jeb. He drove, and she held the flowers, and the kids sat in the back, the younger ones knowing they had to be solemn, but not really sure why. Only Dylan had strong memories of Pat.

Today, she'd come alone. She'd mentioned the date to Dylan yesterday, and when he didn't twig, she decided she'd like to be on her own this year. She could bring Dylan over later, if he wanted.

She hadn't called Jeb, though she knew he'd remember. She was in so much pain today. Pat, Jeb—the loves she'd lost melded together, leaving her a churning mess.

She flipped her turn signal and drove into the cemetery. Each year, the cemetery posted a security guard and a cordon near the grave for the early part of the day, so family, which in other years had included Jeb, could visit in peace. Later, the place would be overrun with fans. As she walked to Pat's grave, Cara felt incredibly alone.

The guard knew her, nodded as she passed. Cara set her flowers in the concrete urn, and spread the blooms out. Then she bowed her head and prayed for her family, for herself. For Jeb.

She heard the muffled crunch of footsteps on the frost-coated grass, and when she opened her eyes she wasn't surprised to see Jeb.

"May I?" He held out a bunch of red and white gerberas.

"Of course."

He put the flowers into the urn along with hers. Cara got down beside him and made them into more of an arrangement. Then they stood, and Jeb said his own silent prayer.

Cara brushed grass from her jeans as she waited for Jeb to finish. She didn't mind that he was here. It was right. Jeb and Pat had been friends forever, and he would always be a part of her life. They needed to be able to stand in the same room, at the same grave, without her disintegrating.

"Cara." Jeb said her name in a low, urgent tone.

She knew what was coming. Because Jeb Stallworth didn't give up, on the track or off. "Jeb, this isn't the time."

"I know you love me," he said. "You can't bury your feelings the way you buried your husband."

She gasped, yet it seemed both profane and right to be having this conversation here. "I can't take another loss."

"I'll give up racing," he said.

Tears started into her eyes. He would do that, for her? Give up the sport that had been his life? He couldn't have told her more clearly how much she meant to him.

"We both know that's not the point." She blew her nose into a tissue. "Racing didn't cause Pat's death. Can you guarantee I'll never lose you?"

"I can guarantee I'll never voluntarily leave you." His eyes were hungry, and he took her hands in his.

"That's not what I asked." She wanted to throw herself into his arms…but even more, she wanted to run away from him and the danger he represented. The danger she might end up with a broken heart all over again.

"Jeb, I *can* bury my feelings. And I will." She detached her hands from his, and took a step backward. Damp grass brushed her ankle where one sock had slipped down. "Please accept my word on this. It's really over."

She held his gaze until he turned away, dashing at his eyes with his hand. She told herself his grief was as much for Pat as for her.

She wanted to howl.

EVER SINCE JEB'S CRASH in Atlanta, Cara had been consumed with a constant desire to see her children. The feeling intensified on Wednesday, as she got into her car after the end of a difficult shift at the hospital. Quickly, she phoned home.

"Everything's great," Michelle, the sitter, informed her.

But Cara couldn't shake a feeling of foreboding as she drove back to the house faster than normal.

"Kids?" She ran inside, glancing wildly around.

"Hi." Michelle picked up her purse, ready to go. "They're watching TV in the den."

Cara managed a perfunctory goodbye before she raced to the den.

She stopped in the doorway. All three kids were sprawled in varying poses on the sectional sofa, watching TV. She clutched the doorjamb as her knees sagged. "Hey, guys."

A chorus of hellos greeted her, though their attention didn't waver from the screen. Then she saw what they were watching. A replay of the Atlanta race.

She felt sick in the pit of her stomach as she walked into the room and sank down on the couch. Lucy immediately snuggled into her. "Mama, we're watching Uncle Jeb."

"And Justin Murphy," Dylan said, naming his new hero.

Cara looked at the lap number in the corner of the screen. Jeb's crash was about ten laps away. "How about we turn this off and go to Maudie's for dinner?"

"We want to watch Uncle Jeb crash," Shane said.

She reached across and squeezed his shoulders. "Honey, crashes aren't entertainment."

Though there were plenty of fans who loved nothing more than a good tangle.

"We want to watch," Shane said again.

Okay, maybe they should all watch it. She could remind herself that although she'd felt empty all day, it was better than watching Jeb crash. Empty had nothing on terrified.

When Bart Branch gained on Jeb, she braced herself. She wanted to yell at the screen, to scream at Jeb to watch out. Her fingers tightened around the hem of Lucy's hoodie.

Bart hit Jeb's car, and she felt almost as bad as she had when it had happened, even though she knew he was fine. Watching it on screen, she saw his struggle to maneuver the car through the crowded field, the other cars that could have hit him, making it worse, before O'Bryan did. Then the TV network replayed it, slow-mo, from about a thousand different angles.

She moaned, quietly enough that the kids didn't hear.

Dylan was cheering as Jeb got out of the car on screen. He pulled off his helmet and waved to the fans, irritated by his forced finish. But not hurt.

Cara tipped her head back against the couch, eyes closed, shivering.

"Are you cold, Mama?" Lucy asked.

She opened her eyes. "Kids, when you saw Jeb crash at the track, were you scared?"

"No," they chorused.

"Not even a tiny bit?"

"Mom, crashes happen all the time in NASCAR," Dylan said patiently. "Dad used to crash."

Yes, and each time her blood had turned to ice in her veins. "Accidents can…your dad died in an accident."

"That was on a boat. Like the cop—the police officer," he amended, correctly interpreting the narrowing of Cara's eyes, "said, it was a million to one chance that tree fell into the river and no one could see it."

Not quite a million to one, but she didn't argue the numbers.

Dylan was watching her. "Were you upset when Uncle Jeb crashed, Mom?"

She nodded.

"Don't be," he advised her. "Uncle Jeb's a great driver. I'm going to be as good as he is one day."

Dismay stole over her. "You mean, on the road?"

Dylan rolled his eyes. "Mom, you know I'm going to race in NASCAR."

He'd always said that when Pat was alive, but as they'd gone to the races less and less, he hadn't mentioned it.

"Sweetie, you might change your mind—"

"I won't," he said. "And Dad said it was okay."

He was building a head of steam, so she let it go. No need to argue about it now—she would just lock him in his room until he turned thirty. Of course, Jeb would say she was trying to make all the rules.

"I love Uncle Jeb," Lucy announced.

Cara's dismay intensified. Lucy barely remembered Pat. Jeb was the nearest thing she'd known to a father.

"I was scared when he crashed," Lucy continued.

"Me, too," Cara said grimly. *On both counts. I love him and I was scared.*

"Did you kiss Uncle Jeb better, Mama?"

Cara blushed. "Uncle Jeb's a big boy, sweetie."

"I was scared he might want to cry, but he couldn't because he's a boy, and no one might kiss him better."

"*That's* why you were scared? Not because he might be hurt?"

Lucy stared at her, confused. She didn't associate race crashes with pain. "Were you there, Mama?" she persisted. "With Uncle Jeb?"

Yes, Cara had been—but she'd been too busy whacking him with her purse to comfort him!

She felt awful. Jeb would have liked some comforting, not because he was injured but because his hopes for the race had been destroyed. She'd been so caught up in her own emotions, she'd ignored his.

And the brief satisfaction of hitting him hadn't lasted. She'd felt no better for her outburst. She'd dumped him, but that hadn't stopped her reliving the terror watching TV just now.

Not being with Jeb when he crashes won't make it any easier to handle. The realization pinned her to the couch, paralyzed her. She could refuse to watch the races, but not knowing would only make it worse.

And no doubt the kids would describe every nudge in gory detail, and she'd be lured to the TV. Where one day she would have to watch some other woman kissing Jeb better.

Now she really did feel sick.

And if the worst did happen…if he had an accident like Pat…could she live with herself, knowing he'd loved her and she'd left him? Knowing she hadn't taken every chance to be with him, to love him back? Imagine being left only with the misery of "what might have been" instead of the joy of "what was."

She clapped a hand over her mouth.

"Are you going to throw up?" Dylan asked, interested.

She opened her fingers a crack to say a muffled, "No."

Her mind churned. Was it too late to put right the mess she'd made? Or had her cowardice driven Jeb away? He'd said her strength was one of the things he loved most about her. Cara groaned. Jeb Stallworth had told her he loved her, and she'd told him to forget it. She remembered the contempt in his eyes. *Please, let him get over that.*

She could call him right now, tell him that she could and would give him all of herself, willingly. But why should he believe her, after the way she'd wimped out?

She needed to prove she was better, braver than the woman who'd walked out on him in Atlanta.

I'll show him. I'll give him concrete, solid proof that I'm willing to do things differently. No turning back, no half measures.

"When are we going to Maudie's?" Shane asked.

Cara kissed his cheek. "I need to make some calls first."

As she left the kids watching TV and went to the kitchen, she prayed it wasn't too late. She pulled the telephone directory from its drawer and began flicking through the pages.

CHAPTER THIRTEEN

EVERY MUSCLE IN JEB'S BODY ACHED. The team had been testing the No. 464 car at Halesboro on Sunday and Monday, since it was an off weekend for the NASCAR Sprint Cup Series. Although there'd been none of the pressure of a race, there was also none of the exhilaration that helped deaden the discomfort. He'd run hundreds of laps, and as he drove the winding roads that led to his house, he could feel every one of them.

I'm getting old.

But not that old. He still had plenty of years of racing left—look at Dean Grosso, who'd finally won the NASCAR Sprint Cup Series championship when he was fifty. Ben Edmonds had several years on Jeb, and Jeb was sure his friend would soon find his groove again, and go on to win more races.

Of course, Jeb would give up NASCAR in a heartbeat if it would convince Cara he was a safe enough bet. But that wasn't going to happen. That was why he'd felt the pain of driving so much today. He didn't have the woman he wanted, the woman who made everything in life better. It hurt.

"So I need to go find someone else," he told himself without enthusiasm.

Yeah, right. He hadn't managed to get over Cara in sixteen years.

As he turned into his driveway and drove up the tree-lined avenue, he glanced at his watch. Eight o'clock. He hadn't eaten. Though he couldn't be bothered, he needed to replenish some of the nutrients he'd lost. There were burgers in the freezer. A couple of burgers, a soak in the hot tub, then bed.

He rounded the bend in the driveway. "What the—?"

His house was a blaze of light. Not just the timed security lighting that came on to convince people the place was occupied, but pretty much every light downstairs.

Cara's SUV was parked at the foot of the front steps.

Was something wrong? One of the kids? Jeb swung to a stop and jumped out of the car, aches forgotten, not bothering to close the door.

He ran inside. "Cara? Kids?"

"Hi, Uncle Jeb." Lucy stood in the entrance hall.

"Lucy." He dropped to a crouch. "What are you doing here?"

She took that as an invitation to throw herself at him and plant a smacking kiss on his mouth. "We came to kiss you better. After your crash at 'Lanta."

Huh, touching. He hugged her. He loved her so much, loved all Pat's kids. "Where's your mom?"

"Come this way," she said importantly.

But in the living room, it wasn't Cara waiting for him, but Shane.

"You and I need to talk, Uncle Jeb," he announced. "Man to man."

The kid was so cute, Jeb almost laughed out loud. But Shane had something going on, his face serious. Instead of hugging him, Jeb shook his hand…which made Shane wiggle with excitement.

Jeb registered the aroma of food cooking. Something delicious. And beyond the living room, he saw the dining table set for two, with a tablecloth and candles. And a pot of mustard.

The aches and pains of the day faded away.

Jeb sat on the couch; Shane perched on the coffee table in front of him. "We need a new dad," he announced.

"I couldn't agree more," Jeb said. "Your real dad will always be in your heart, but you need a new one around the house, right?"

"Right. And Mom needs a new husband. Will you do it?" Shane asked. "Will you be our dad and Mom's husband?"

Jeb felt faintly indignant that Cara thought she had to use the kids to get at him. Didn't she know he'd do anything if it meant he ended up with her love?

"I'd be honored," Jeb said. And when Shane looked confused, "You bet, I'd love to."

Shane relaxed. "We need to shake hands again. That way you don't get to change your mind."

"No chance of that, buddy." Jeb sealed the deal with a handshake, then kissed Shane. "It's time I talked to your mom, don't you think?" Now, he just had to find Cara and make it official, so she couldn't back out, either.

"Not yet." Shane jumped off the coffee table and called, "Dylan!"

Jeb stifled a groan when Dylan appeared. Good thing he loved the little squirts, or he'd be insane with impatience. "What have you got for me, Dylan?"

Dylan handed him a cold beer.

"Bribery, great idea," Jeb approved. "But not necessary in this case." He took a courtesy swig of the beer. "I really need to get to your mom."

"Are you going to marry her?" Dylan asked.

"You bet." *If I ever get near her.*

"She can be a pain sometimes."

"It's okay, I like pains." Including the three who were stopping him getting to the woman he loved.

"She has lots of rules," Dylan warned.

"Rules are good, they let you know what's the right thing. NASCAR has rules." No way could the kid argue with that. He took a step toward the kitchen.

"Mom's given me some rules for you." Dylan held up a folded sheet of paper.

Jeb stopped, his heart plummeting. Surely Cara didn't still have some crazy idea they could be together but separate. Like, she couldn't come to races, and the kids couldn't cut school…. Like how far Jeb could "intrude" on her life.

With trepidation, he took the paper, unfolded it. Only two rules:

1. Love me Always.

2. Let me love you always.

Jeb stared at the page, his heart swelling.

"Are they okay?" Dylan asked. "Because if it's about bedtime, you can negotiate."

It was about bedtime and a whole lot more. Jeb beamed at Dylan. Soon to be his son. "I can do this."

He waved the paper. "But now, you need to do something for me. Keep your brother and sister out here. I need some private time with your mom."

"Sure thing." Dylan went to give orders to his siblings.

Jeb escaped to the kitchen and closed the door behind him. Cara stood in the middle of the room, fingers laced.

"Hi." She smiled shyly.

She wore cowboy boots, a denim skirt and a see-through blouse…with a modest camisole beneath. She looked like the woman of his dreams.

Jeb took her in his arms, tugged her against him, went deep into her mouth. He ran his hands over her delectable curves, and her response was everything he'd wanted. Pure and passionate.

When he lifted his head, she said, "I take it my rules are acceptable?"

"Perfect." He kissed her again. "Just like you." He glanced at the island, cluttered with makeup, magazines and kids' homework. "You look as if you live here."

To his surprise, she blushed. "Actually, I do. The kids and I do."

He gaped. "You're moving in?" Something brushed against his ankle, and he glanced down. "Is that your *cat?*"

"I put my house on the market on Friday and had an offer today. The Realtor told me there'd be no difficulty selling the former home of a NASCAR legend, and she was right."

"I can't believe you did that. You love that place."

He brushed a strand of hair off her forehead, regarding her with concern.

"It was a great home for me and Pat, but I'm with you now. I wanted you to know for sure that I'm all yours. Completely."

"Point taken." He kissed her. "Thank you."

"There's more," she said.

He braced himself.

"I quit my job. I told them I'm available for relief work, any time it doesn't conflict with a race weekend."

"Cara…" Jeb choked up. "Are you sure?"

"I'll still have plenty of hours at the hospital, they're desperate for temp nurses. But it won't interfere with us."

"Oh, man, I'm the luckiest guy in the world."

"I'm not done yet."

"Let me guess…you have some new lingerie to show me?" he said hopefully.

She blushed beautifully as she swatted him. "I took the kids out of school and signed on for home-schooling. Whether you like it or not, that motor home of yours will be mighty crowded come race weekend."

Jeb stared at her.

"Jeb?" Her voice quivered. "I guess I did go a little overboard. I just wanted you to know—"

"That you're giving this your all. I get it loud and clear, honey."

"It may not be easy," she said. "I know you love the kids, but having three of them around full-time, being their dad…"

"I can't wait," he assured her. "But if you think three kids is a problem, we can always make it four or five."

She laughed, and kissed him.

"I DON'T KNOW what I did to deserve this," he said some time later, "but you've made me nearly the happiest man on the planet."

"Nearly?" she said, half tremulous, half indignant.

"One more thing and I'll officially be the happiest."

Cara folded her arms and glared at him. Which was difficult to pull off, as mushy and madly in love as she felt. Still, she couldn't let Jeb think he called all the shots. "Explain," she ordered.

"Tomorrow, we drive to Tennessee with the kids and we get married," he said. "There's no waiting period, no blood test. All we have to do is show up and say we'll love each other forever." He paused. "Or is it too soon? It's sure not for me, but, honey, if you want a big wedding, all the trimmings…or if you just want to wait a while, that's fine." He looked so disappointed at the thought, she laughed. Her noble NASCAR driver.

"Are you kidding? I'm not sure tomorrow is soon enough." And she pressed her mouth to his.

* * * * *

HARLEQUIN®

A Romance

FOR EVERY MOOD™

Spotlight on
Heart & Home

Heartwarming romances
where love can happen
right when you least expect it.

See the next page to enjoy a sneak peek
from Silhouette Special Edition®,
a Heart and Home series.

CATHHSSE10

*Introducing McFARLANE'S PERFECT BRIDE
by USA TODAY bestselling author Christine Rimmer,
from Silhouette Special Edition®.*

Entranced. Captivated. Enchanted.

Connor sat across the table from Tori Jones and couldn't help thinking that those words exactly described what effect the small-town schoolteacher had on him. He might as well stop trying to tell himself he wasn't interested. He was powerfully drawn to her.

Clearly, he should have dated more when he was younger.

There had been a couple of other women since Jennifer had walked out on him. But he had never been entranced. Or captivated. Or enchanted.

Until now.

He wanted her—*her,* Tori Jones, in particular. Not just someone suitably attractive and well-bred, as Jennifer had been. Not just someone sophisticated, sexually exciting and discreet, which pretty much described the two women he'd dated after his marriage crashed and burned.

It came to him that he...he *liked* this woman. And that was new to him. He liked her quick wit, her wisdom and her big heart. He liked the passion in her voice when she talked about things she believed in.

He liked *her.* And suddenly it mattered all out of proportion that she might like him, too.

Was he losing it? He couldn't help but wonder. Was he cracking under the strain—of the soured economy, the McFarlane House setbacks, his divorce, the scary changes in his son? Of the changes he'd decided he needed to make in his life and himself?

Strangely, right then, on his first date with Tori Jones, he didn't care if he just might be going over the edge. He was having a great time—having *fun,* of all things—and he didn't want it to end.

Is Connor finally able to admit his feelings to Tori, and are they reciprocated?
Find out in McFARLANE'S PERFECT BRIDE
by USA TODAY bestselling author Christine Rimmer.
Available July 2010,
only from Silhouette Special Edition®.

Copyright © 2010 by Christine Reynolds

SSEEXP0710

Love Inspired®

Bestselling author

JILLIAN HART

launches a brand-new continuity

ALASKAN *Bride* RUSH

*Women are flocking to the land of the Midnight Sun
with marriage on their minds.*

A tiny town full of churchgoing, marriage-minded men? For
Karenna Digby Treasure Creek sounds like a dream come true.
Until she's stranded at the ranch of search-and-rescue guide
Gage Parker, who is *not* looking for love. But can she *guide* her
Klondike hero on the greatest adventure of all—love?

KLONDIKE HERO

*Available in July
wherever books are sold.*

Steeple
Hill®
LI87608

www.SteepleHill.com

HARLEQUIN®

Super Romance®

Top *author*

Janice Kay Johnson

*brings readers a heartwarming
small-town story*

with

CHARLOTTE'S HOMECOMING

After their father is badly injured on the farm, Faith Russell calls her estranged twin sister, Charlotte, to return to the small rural town she escaped so many years ago. When Charlotte falls for Gray Van Dusen, the handsome town mayor, her feelings of home begin to change. As the relationship grows, will Charlotte finally realize that there is no better place than *home?*

*Available in July
wherever books are sold.*

www.eHarlequin.com

HSR71644

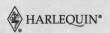

INTRIGUE

**BESTSELLING
HARLEQUIN INTRIGUE AUTHOR**

DEBRA WEBB

**INTRODUCES THE LATEST
COLBY AGENCY SPIN-OFF**

MERGER

No one or nothing would stand in the way
of an Equalizer agent…but every Colby agent
is a force to be reckoned with.

Look for
COLBY CONTROL—*July*
COLBY VELOCITY—*August*

www.eHarlequin.com   HI69483

Stay up-to-date on all your romance-reading news with the brand-new Harlequin *Inside Romance!*

The Harlequin *Inside Romance* is a **FREE** quarterly newsletter highlighting our upcoming series releases and promotions!

Click on the *Inside Romance* link on the front page of www.eHarlequin.com or e-mail us at InsideRomance@Harlequin.ca to sign up to receive your FREE newsletter today!

You can also subscribe by writing to us at: HARLEQUIN BOOKS
Attention: Customer Service Department
P.O. Box 9057, Buffalo, NY 14269-9057

Please allow 4-6 weeks for delivery of the first issue by mail.

IRNBPAQ309